THE DRAGON KINGS

OBSIDIAN

BOOK I

KIMBERLY LOTH

Cover design by Rebecca Frank

Interior design by Colleen Sheehan of Write. Dream. Repeat. Book
Design

For Mandy, Kristin, and Karen
For believing in me from the very beginning

PROLOGUE

TRAVIS SPRINGS USUALLY didn't hike in the national parks. He preferred his mountains dragon free, thank you very much, but his buddies told him this hike was safe and worth the risk.

Everyone knew the best hikes were in the national parks, and Travis figured he'd have to get over his aversion to dragons if he was going to be serious about climbing mountains.

The scenery was breathtaking. The valley below him shimmered in greens and yellows. Not to mention the mist that rose from the steam vents covering the entire Yellowstone floor.

He stopped to take a drink. According to the map, he was a quarter of a mile from the top. This was one of the smaller mountains, and so it had to be safe. It was rumored that the dragons in Yellowstone typically didn't come down from the very top of the tallest peaks.

Travis looked up and saw a gold speck high in the sky. He shivered and watched the path as he walked. In his head, he repeated words he read and heard over the last few weeks. Dragons didn't eat people. There were no documented cases. His fear was irrational, but then again most fears were.

He concentrated on the ground and climbed up the rocky terrain. After about twenty minutes, he finally made it to the top.

Travis refused to look up at the sky and instead surveyed the valley below him. In the distance, a herd of buffalo grazed in the plains. He took a few deep breaths and felt his fear subside. He'd been silly.

He took a chance and peeked at the sky. The speck looked closer, and his stomach clenched. But then he reminded himself that because he reached the top, the speck would obviously be closer.

Travis's hands shook as he took a drink of his water. He convinced himself that he'd spend fifteen minutes or so and then head back down. But he didn't waste all day climbing to the top, just to race to the bottom.

Travis dug in his bag and found his camera.

The air around him suddenly felt ten degrees warmer. Sweat beaded on Travis's forehead. A hot wind whooshed from above him. He clutched at his camera and looked up.

The golden underbelly of the dragon was only about ten feet above him, flying over him quickly. The thing had to be a hundred feet long from the snout to the tip of its tail. Travis felt his jeans go wet. If he lived to tell this tale, he'd leave out that detail. He reminded himself to breathe.

As fast as it had come, it was gone. Travis couldn't move. He watched the dragon turn and head back toward him. Travis clutched the camera and took a picture as the dragon opened its wide mouth. Its teeth were three feet long and wicked sharp.

Seconds before the jaws clamped down on him, he dropped the camera. The air from the dragon's throat blistered his skin, but it didn't spew fire. Travis's final thought was, *What a horrible way to die.*

As the dragon flew away, thoroughly pleased with his meal, he didn't realize he left behind not one, but two souvenirs. The camera.

And a foot.

CHAPTER 1

T HE SEA'S SALTY air reached into the hideout and woke Obsidian. Not ready to get up, he stretched his wing, feeling for Skye. Instead of finding her warmth, he met the grimy cave floor. A shot of panic zipped from his horns to his tail.

She always woke him before she got up. Opening his eyes, he searched for her. She sat near the entrance to the cave, staring over the ocean, the early morning sunlight reflecting off her sapphire scales.

She swiveled her neck and narrowed her eyes. Tears flowed down her ice-blue snout and over her smooth underbelly, forming a pool between her feet. She unfurled her great wings and shook her head, splattering teardrops on the walls.

Skye never cried, at least not in the hundred and sixty-two years they'd been together. Her occasional tantrums caused entire forests to disappear and caves to collapse, but her silver eyes always remained dry. Obsidian moved forward to comfort her, longing to understand why she wept.

Stop, she shrieked in his mind.

Her sorrow became his. Obsidian took three deep breaths and tried to identify her emotions. He wanted the easy free flow of feelings they often shared, but he could barely keep his mind straight with the turmoil.

As royal dragons, they could feel the emotions of those around them, a gift Obsidian usually appreciated. Except in situations like this. Now he wished for the gift of the canyon dragons, who could probe minds.

He forced her feelings away, focusing on peace and quiet. When he pushed out all her sadness, he continued toward her, convinced if he were near her, she would calm down.

Silvery blue flames erupted from her jaw. Obsidian ducked to avoid being singed, his mental block faltering, and a wave of desolation flooded his body. He shook, and his eyes watered. He squeezed them shut, fighting again to regain control of his emotions. He had to put a stop to this.

What's wrong? he asked and crept closer.

Folding her wings, she moved her body toward the front of the cave. Her head struck the ceiling, stripping off the stalactites. Obsidian winced for her. The light disappeared as her body filled the opening, and smoke engulfed the enclosed space.

Are you upset about last night? Obsidian asked. They'd argued about the future, a future she thought was in jeopardy.

She didn't answer. He took advantage of the darkness and moved to her, running the side of his jaw along her neck, something that always pleased her. She jerked, and he recoiled, her rejection stinging.

Back off. I can't be near you. Her voice, normally sweet in his head, was now icy and cold.

Skye, he whispered, trying to understand.

I mean it, Obsidian. Leave me alone.

The distance she created was unnerving. Curse the rules he had to follow. Once again he wished he had been born into one of the different dragon races or at a different time. If that had been the case, their future would be sure. But he'd been born a royal dragon, a possible heir to the throne, and so far, his life was dictated for him.

We could run away. Find the mountains in South Africa where the council could never find us. In a few years, the new king will be crowned, and we'll come back. Obsidian knew that as soon as the king was chosen, he was off the hook.

She shook, her wings rustling and her tail swishing. *That won't work. Not now. Two days ago we could've done that, but not today. You should go and present yourself to the council.*

Becoming human is not urgent. I'll wait. I can't stand to see you like this.

You can't wait! she roared.

Skye collapsed and heaved with sobs. Obsidian draped his neck across her, hating the rules he was bound to. Royal dragons had to go through the human experience before their five hundredth birthday. He put it off because he treasured the time with Skye. Plus, he hated his human form. They had to take it on occasionally in their lessons, but he'd never gone out among the real humans.

You're going to leave me. We'll never be bonded, she whimpered.

Obsidian sighed. This was absurd. *I only have to be human for ten years. Maybe less if I finish everything early. We'll be bonded as soon as I'm done. You know this.*

She pulled out from underneath him and spun around. *Don't make promises you can't keep, Your Majesty.* She spat out the words and leapt from the ledge of the cave, soaring over the sea. Her silver wings shimmered in the sunlight, her body still heaving as she flew south.

Obsidian's entire body tensed. He dug his claws into the cave floor. He'd never been called Your Majesty. He was a royal dragon, but he wasn't the king. He closed his eyes and hurtled into the biting wind, heading north.

Birds twittered. An airplane passed high above, and the waves of the ocean crashed below. Obsidian turned inland, heading for a quieter setting, drifting through the air and landing at the edge of a lake.

The sharp scent of pine stung his nostrils. He cracked his eyelids a sliver, searching for his reflection. When he found it, his insides turned cold. His body, a glittering gold for four centuries, was now a deep coal black.

Obsidian sat on the bank staring at his new self, disgusted. In the sunlight he could still see some gold, but mostly he was darker than the night sky. He hated what it meant for him. Skye left because she understood that in spite of all the plans they made, the inevitable had come to pass. They would never be together again.

Obsidian's heart ached. His mate would now be chosen for him, and Skye would never qualify. He sniffed and watched the black smoke float above him. His smoke used to be gold. He was glad he never sealed himself to her because then they both would've been killed as soon as he turned black.

They'd had their silly little fantasies of what life would be like after he fulfilled his duties. Once one of his brothers was chosen, most likely Prometheus, he would have finally allowed himself to be sealed to her. Their children raised by the sea. Now Skye would never become his mate, because *he* had been selected.

Dragons came in many colors—silver, gold, red, blue, orange, yellow, brown, and purple. But only one dragon was black.

The king.

CHAPTER 2

ASPEN'S EYES FLASHED opened and settled on the picture of a rust-colored dragon hanging above her bed. Her hands shook as she pushed her hair out of her face. It was just a dream, no biggie. Her right hand ached. Weird. She looked at it and found her knuckles red.

Someone spewed curses from the other side of her room. She sprung out of bed, ready for a fight. Her dad danced around the room holding his eye. She must've hit him when she woke up. Damn nightmares. Damn Marc. Why'd he haunt her after all these years?

"Oh, Dad, I'm sorry. I was having a bad dream." Aspen leaned over, picked up his ranger hat, and handed it to him.

"It's okay. Next time remind me to yell from the door."

She chuckled, still trying to get a good look at his face. "Sure, I'll remember to do that while I'm sleeping."

He grinned, and she touched the reddening skin around his eye. "That's going to bruise. What are you going to tell them at work? That your seventeen-year-old daughter beat you up?"

"Nah, I'll come up with a better story. I know it's early, but I'm heading to work, and I wanted to make sure you were packed."

Aspen squirmed. "Uh, not exactly. But I'll pack tonight, I swear."

"We leave for Hawaii first thing tomorrow morning. Why not pack now?" He twirled his hat in his hand, smiling. He was just trying to get her to ask permission. Something she didn't do on a regular basis.

"Because I'm going rappelling, but I promise it'll get done."

"Aspen, we missed our flight last time because you hadn't packed."

"I know, but that was just California. This is Hawaii."

He winked and left the room, giving her that "Yeah, sure" look. He wasn't the best at enforcing rules, and he never stayed mad at her long, even when she royally screwed up. He didn't need to worry. She might end up with nothing more than a bathing suit, toothbrush, and camera shoved in her backpack, but she was getting on that plane. It was Hawaii for crying out loud.

Aspen flitted around her room for a little bit. She dug out every single one of her cameras and lined them up on her dresser. It was unrealistic to take them all, but she'd never seen the blood-red dragons that flew around the volcanoes in Hawaii. She'd seen a few pictures, but no one was as good as she was at capturing them. Hell, most people didn't dare to get that close to the dragons. Even those who liked them.

Aspen's whole goal in life was to become the Crocodile Hunter of dragons. But that would never happen if she stayed in her room packing on a perfectly good Thursday morning. She could pack tonight when the dragons were harder to spot. The clock read quarter to nine. If much more time passed, she'd spend an hour in traffic. Aspen threw on a pair of jeans, found her rappelling pack, and grabbed a banana before heading out the door.

Yellowstone crawled with tourists during the summer. Aspen was glad the season was almost over and she could have the park to herself again. Her jeep wove carefully in and out of motor homes and mini-vans. She hoped she wouldn't come across the all too frequent buffalo-in-the-road traffic jam. After a few miles, she found a hidden intersection with a small sign labeled "Authorized Personnel Only" next to a steep dirt road. She turned off the highway onto the road, kicking up a cloud of dirt. She sort of was authorized personnel—one of the advantages of being the daughter of two park rangers. All the rangers knew her, and if she got caught, they'd just laugh and tell her she was wasting her time. The golden dragons in this park were much harder to photograph because they never flew close to the ground. But she still tried. As she climbed the mountain, her skin tingled with excitement. This place was her best shot because last week she spotted footprints.

When she was four, Aspen met an actual dragon. Ever since then, she had to settle for shooting them in flight. Which wasn't bad, but she'd give anything to be face-to-face with one again. This road led to the best chance of that happening.

She put the jeep in four-wheel drive to navigate the steep incline. The hair on the back of her neck rose. Her eyes flicked up to the rear-view mirror, but the only thing behind her was dust from her tires.

A dark shadow passed in front of the car, and she slammed on the brakes, spraying gravel and rocks into the brush. The jeep slid backwards. She pushed it into first gear and accelerated, trying to keep it from sliding. The ascent was slow, having lost all momentum. The rocky road went through a stand of pine trees. The shadow loomed larger as she moved closer to the top of the hill. She wanted to check out the sky, but the narrow road demanded all of her attention.

The jeep crested the hill, and the rocky road gave way to a large plateau. On the far side, the grass ended, revealing jagged rocks and a cliff.

Another shadow passed over the car, not just a shapeless cloud, but a shadow with wings. Aspen scrambled out of the car and looked up. The sun blinded her, and all she could see was a dark mass.

She rushed to open the hatch and flung aside her gear in search of her rappelling pack. She found it. It was the one with her GoPro inside. She dug through the bag, tossing out granola bars and water bottles, but the camera was nowhere to be found. She thought back to this morning, and her heart sank. The camera was sitting on her dresser—waiting to be packed. Damn her foresight for Hawaii.

She backed up and shielded her eyes, searching the skies. There wasn't a dragon in sight. Not even way up among the clouds where the usual golden and silver specks flew. She'd just seen him.

The ground shook, and she stumbled, trying not to fall. She spun around. Sitting not ten feet from her was a dragon.

CHAPTER 3

A GORGEOUS, HUMONGOUS BLACK dragon. Aspen's pulse raced, and a huge smile formed on her lips. She needed her freaking camera. She didn't dare move, afraid he would fly away.

She'd never seen a black dragon before. He moved toward her until his gigantic head was nearly above her. Twenty feet up, but still right overhead. His wings quivered, and his jaw opened, revealing teeth as long as swords. Silvery black flames erupted from his throat. The forest behind her disappeared. He didn't set it on fire; he disintegrated it, leaving only smoking ash-covered stumps.

He closed his mouth and brought his head down. Aspen's heart fluttered, and she took a small step backwards. Her palms began to sweat. He turned his neck so she could look straight into his eye, the sea-blue disk as large as her upper body. His lids clicked every time he blinked. His eyes were haunted, like he was carrying the weight of the world.

Aspen traced one of the scales under his eye, marveling at the feel of it on her fingertips. She inhaled. He smelled like a campfire. A sharp pain stung her ankle, almost like a snakebite, and she jerked her hand away in surprise. As she lifted her foot up and looked down, the dragon jumped. Aspen took a few steps back in an effort to stay upright. His wings opened, and he hovered for a few seconds. Then he was gone.

She'd waited years to come face-to-face with a dragon and could've done a thousand different things. Instead, she stood there like a dumbass. The highlight of her life and it was over in thirty seconds.

Her ankle burned. It had to be a snakebite, and she cursed herself for being the third person in the history of Yellowstone to be bit by a prairie rattler. She hobbled back to the car, knowing the snake was long gone. Surely the reptile had warned her, but she was so in love with the sight in front of her that she ignored the ground.

This would put a damper on the Hawaii trip. Aspen's sister was going to kill her. She called at least three times a day for the last two weeks. Her parents wouldn't be happy about this latest development either.

The only hope was that it was a dry bite with no venom. Which was possible but not probable. Considering how bad her ankle burned, she wouldn't be that lucky.

This was the third time she'd been bit. The first had been a cottonmouth in Florida—a dry bite. The second had been a cobra, and that was just a result of stupidity. She was twelve and wanted to pet it, assuming since it was in a glass cage it wouldn't strike. She ended up in the hospital for a week.

She peeled away her sock in search of two tiny dots. Instead, a swirl of black covered her ankle. She gasped.

The intricate inch-wide tattoo looped and swished, encircling her entire ankle. The pattern was deliberate, a marking of some kind. Where on earth had that come from? She thought for a minute of what would suddenly cause a tattoo to appear on her ankle. Unless it hadn't suddenly appeared. Had she done something dumb the night before? She thought about the evening and couldn't find any gaps.

Could it have been the dragon? She never heard a dragon marking a person before. Then again, as far as she knew, no one ever got close enough to a dragon to touch one. Did he mark her so he could find her, or was it something that just happened?

She looked up again and watched the black speck fly over Eagles Peak. Then she quickly slammed the hatch shut and got in her jeep. Rappelling would fall flat compared to touching a dragon. She headed his direction, determined to find him again.

Aspen drove for hours, not finding even a hint he had been around. Tourists shivered when she asked them if they saw the black dragon. One young mother gave her a ten-minute lecture on politeness when her kid burst into tears and screamed about wanting to go home. The cloud-free sky contained not one speck of black. Though several gold and silver dots glittered high in the sky.

Around midnight, Aspen accepted the darkness wouldn't make it any easier to spot him, and so she went home. Everyone in the house was asleep, which was odd because normally Rowan, her twin brother, stayed up late. She snuck into her room and closed the door with a soft click. The floor was difficult to navigate in the dark with clothes and climbing gear strung everywhere.

She tripped and cursed silently, not wanting to wake anyone and draw attention to her late entry. After successfully making it to her bed, she turned on the light on her nightstand and peeled away her socks. In the dim light the tattoo looked more mysterious and ethereal. It was bigger than she originally thought, more like two inches wide, with an occasional loop escaping the careful pattern.

Aspen's parents would be livid. They were amazingly cool about a lot of things. She couldn't remember the last time she spent a weekend at home. But unlike some of her friends with similarly cool parents, she did not spend the time passed out from alcohol. She spent her time in the backcountry camping, or crashed on the bunks at the airport so she could get an early start skydiving.

But her parents did have a few rules to keep this freedom.

Rule number six: no tattoos or body piercings. And Mom would laugh if she said she was marked by a dragon. She'd think Aspen broke rule number two: no drugs. Which of course, she hadn't. Well, except once, but that was a huge mistake that tied in directly with rule number one. Funny, how sex and drugs often went together. And no, her parents didn't say no sex. They said, "Take your birth control pills." She still took her pills, but she didn't see the point now. Sex was in the past, along with the drugs.

When combined, they led to the worst two days of her life. Which involved Marc and her frequent nightmares.

She kept her face free of piercings and her body inkless. She stayed away from drugs and took her pills. And she checked in with her folks every twenty-four hours or so. Less in the summer.

The dragon marking would have to remain a secret. No flip-flops in Hawaii. She'd have to stick to scuba diving and volcano climbing. After a while, she found a clean pair of socks and drifted into dreamland filled with gigantic black dragons and sea-blue eyes.

She didn't set her alarm, Hawaii forgotten.

CHAPTER 4

BECOMING THE DRAGON king had always been a possibility; Obsidian never thought it would become reality. Five of them were potential heirs: Kingston the pious, Raja the realist, Marcellus the arrogant, Prometheus the leader, and Obsidian the slacker. They spent years studying both their own history and human history, because royalty must walk the line between both worlds. The king always referred to the five of them as brothers even though they all came from different parents. He hoped it would instill a sense of family between them instead of competition because it was up to the gods who became king—nothing they did could influence who was chosen.

Each one of them took a turn completing their human experience. Kingston and Raja were always on Obsidian's case, constantly asking when he would be ready. He never saw the point because they all knew Prometheus would be the next king. Why bother? Obsidian played along with all the rules. Except that one. He hated his human form, taking it only when they were forced to read. Dragons could do a lot of things, but reading was difficult when the books were so small.

Why would he subject himself to ten years of that wretched state? Humans were small and vulnerable. He couldn't bear the thought of being like that for so long. Raja argued that it was his duty.

Ice formed on his wings, forcing him to lower his altitude. Prometheus would hate him. He spent the last three months training by the king's side, while His Majesty transitioned from this world to the next. Everyone expected Prometheus to take the throne. Especially Obsidian. Prometheus was his best friend and the most suited for the job.

Obsidian thought back to the girl on the mountainside. Her pure excitement still flowed through his veins, even remembering all that had taken him there. It made this all bearable—the kingship, his ten-year hiatus from the dragon world, Skye, everything. He had hope. Hope that being human would not be horrible, that Prometheus would forgive him, and Skye would be happy. Strange though, as he flew home, his focus was not on Skye, but on the girl in the field.

Raja met Obsidian at the entrance to the king's cave.

Where are the others? Obsidian asked.

Marcellus and Kingston are with the body, waiting for you. Prometheus took off right after the rest of us arrived. He said to go ahead and perform the requiem without him.

Do you know where he was heading?

No. Come, we must perform the ritual, and then you must meet with the council.

The king was stretched out on the floor, his black body faded back to gold. He looked peaceful. Obsidian took his position at the deceased king's head. Marcellus sat at the rear, and Raja and Kingston each took a side. Obsidian would go last. Marcellus began.

He opened his jaw wide and let out a jet of golden flame. It engulfed the tail, and the body of the king began to disappear. Raja and Kingston joined Marcellus when he reached the flank. The gold light was blinding. Soon all that was left was the king's head. All three cut off their flames and waited. Obsidian looked at the face of his king one last time. A jet of black flames escaped him, and the king was gone. They each let out another blast of flame, and a gold gem appeared where the ashes had been. It would sit in the king's hall with the rest of the dead kings.

They sat in silence for a moment.

Obsidian, it's time to see the council, Raja said.

Obsidian didn't answer him but flew down the hall. The walls were covered with ruby gemstones. Torches with multi-colored flames lit the path. A sudden realization hit Obsidian—this was his hall now. His cave. He planned to change the gemstones to sapphires. The ruby stones looked too much like blood.

The council met in a deep pit. It was large enough to hold a hundred dragons. In Obsidian's lifetime, there had never been a need to hold such a meeting. Now only seven dragons inhabited the space. It was wide and well lit.

Obsidian flew down to meet with them. Their eyes followed him. When he landed, they all bowed. The bow was unnecessary. They all knew he had no power at that point. They held the power and could have him killed if it was their wish.

A menacing voice entered his head. *Foolish dragon. You knew this was a possibility, yet you made no effort to be ready. Now you put us all at risk while you make your preparations.*

Anasazi, the large orange canyon dragon, sneered at him.

Obsidian's sister answered before Obsidian had a chance. *Be nice. I'm sure he's still in shock. Obsidian, the time has come for you to complete your human experience. When it is over, you will take the throne as a proper king. We all know that you becoming king wasn't the ideal situation. But the Gods have chosen you. I see no reason to prolong this. Are you ready?*

Obsidian sat tall and looked at each member of the council. From the tiny underground dragon to the monstrous white dragon.

I'm ready.

CHAPTER 5

OBSIDIAN SQUEEZED HIS eyes, forcing them to stay closed. But he still couldn't sleep. He kicked off the blanket and rolled over, the bed sinking. Air, he needed air, and a nice rock floor. The quest for sleep was pointless. The whole house was squishy, the floor, the bed, the chairs. The only rock he could find was the kitchen counter.

Covered in dying vines, the battered brick manor, home to many dragons during their human experiences, had been empty for years. Obsidian's house was bigger than most caves he'd lived in. Ironic since he was smaller than he had ever been. In the last few weeks, a crew updated the interior with all the modern conveniences but left the outside untouched. The inside of the house blinked, flashed, buzzed, and emitted noises like dying birds. It smelled horrible, unnatural. Obsidian missed the quiet of the forests, the fragrance of the wildflowers, and the companionship of Skye. Her absence left him empty.

A door slammed somewhere in the house. It didn't worry him. He assumed it was still some of the crew updating the house, or his mentor. He abandoned the many flashing boxes and went to the bookshelf, hoping to find something that could keep him occupied until his mentor showed up. He crouched down to look at the books on the bottom shelf.

His fists clenched unconsciously, and anger flared in his chest. The feeling was not his own. He turned. Prometheus stood next to the door, his hands gripping the frame.

Look, Obsidian said, standing up. *I understand you are angry.*

"Angry? You think I'm angry? You stole my future." Prometheus stalked toward Obsidian, his fist raised. The hand came toward Obsidian's face with blinding speed. He registered pain as it connected with his jaw. Then he saw blackness.

"Obsidian…Obsidian? You okay?" Prometheus's face swam into view, his blonde dreadlocks tickling Obsidian's nose.

"Um yeah, I think so. What was that for?"

Prometheus held out his hand. Obsidian grabbed it, and Prometheus pulled him up.

"You sure you're okay?"

"Of course."

"Good," he said and punched Obsidian again. His nose exploded with blood.

"Why do you keep doing that?" Obsidian held his nose with both hands, the metallic taste draining down the back of his throat.

Prometheus stood there, his chest rising and falling. His hands were up near his face, waiting.

"Fight back." Prometheus punched Obsidian in the stomach, causing him to double over. "Hit me back."

Prometheus's rapid breath reverberated in Obsidian's ears. He stood straight, still gripping his nose, the blood trailing through his fingers. His jaw ached, his nose throbbed, and his stomach felt like he'd eaten a live bear, but with each punch he could feel Prometheus's anger subside a little.

"Come on." Prometheus motioned with his hands. "Fight me."

"No," Obsidian said, pushing past him to get to the bathroom.

What was Prometheus doing here? The only dragon Obsidian was supposed to have contact with was his mentor. Obsidian was under the impression that his mentor would be his sister or one of his parents. He washed the blood off his face and tried not to look at his swollen features in the mirror. Prometheus hated him, and he could do nothing about it.

When Obsidian walked back into his room, Prometheus sat at the desk pushing buttons on several different boxes, which whirred and blinked and flashed.

"I'm sorry," he said, "but, dude, next time someone hits you like that, you need to hit them back, 'kay?"

"Uh, sure," Obsidian said, confused by some of his words. Prometheus didn't look up, but his fingers were flying across the board in front of the screen.

"What are you doing here?"

"I'm your mentor. Ten more years in this glorious body." Prometheus was not happy about anything right now. Obsidian could sense his sarcasm.

"Why did you hit me anyway?" Obsidian asked.

"I'm pissed as hell that you're king. It's not your fault, but I feel a little better now. Don't you?"

"No."

"Why not?"

"My face feels like it exploded."

Prometheus surveyed Obsidian for a minute. "Yeah, sorry about that. It'll heal quickly. You're a dragon."

"Not right now. Remind me again how long I have to do this."

"Ten years give or take. Not that long really. Seriously, calm down."

"I'm good at being a dragon. I understand how my world works. This," Obsidian said, gesturing around his room. "This is all new. I don't understand any of it, and I have no idea how to interact with them. On top of all that, I'm king, which is something I never wanted."

"Dude, chill. You're gonna be fine. Yeah, high school sucks, but you've only got to go through a year of it. College is much better.

Except the girls don't understand why we won't mate with them."
He smiled. "But bro, that is a lesson for another night." He whirled
around in his chair. "I'll teach you everything I know. Oh, and hey,
don't call me Prometheus either. Humans like simple names. I'm
Theo, and you're Sid."

Obsidian struggled to make sense of his words. Chill, girls, mating,
dude, bro, Sid. He knew Prometheus finished the human experience
in Laguna Beach about six months ago, but he didn't understand how
he could be so different.

Your Human Years was a book that listed all of the things that must be
done during the ten years a dragon spent as a human. From the start
of the human race, dragons had kept this book. The list ranged from
the mundane—learn how to boil water, to the outrageous—discov-
er the stench of the sewer. From simple—have a conversation on a
telephone, to complex—get a college degree. Every dragon who went
through the human experience added to the list. Some only listed one
or two new things, and others added pages. This list was thousands of
entries long.

All royal dragons had to go through the human experience since
they were the liaisons between the dragons and the humans. They had
to know how to communicate with them and relate to their ways of
thinking. Sid had put off his own experience, but knew it was eventually inevitable. He didn't expect to be king though. That changed how
his experience would go. He'd be watched like a hawk.

Sid closed his eyes and put his finger on a random spot in the book.
"Get a Job."

Gardiner, Montana, a small town designed for tourists, sat just outside the north gate of Yellowstone. Sid's driver took him into town.
Once they hit Main Street, Sid asked him to stop so he could walk.

Several signs hung in quirky shops advertising "closing for the season, everything 50% off."

"Wait here. I'll be back in a bit."

The driver nodded.

Sid wandered around for a while, observing the people. He often found conflicting feelings existing within the same human. A couple across the street argued. She had tears rolling down her face, and he clenched his fists. The girl put her hands on his chest and pushed. Sid could feel anger, hatred, and rage coming from them. Yet underlying that was a form a love. He walked away shaking his head.

Sid looked for the signs that Theo told him about: "Help Wanted" and "Now Hiring." After a quarter of a mile, the strip of shops ended, and enormous old houses began. Most had signs outside advertising their business. Lawyers, dentists, accountants, etc.

He spotted one on an enormous house with two blue turrets that framed a whitewashed porch. The sign hanging over the porch read "The Purple Dragon." Seemed like a good enough omen. The screen door slammed behind him as he walked inside. An intense bitter smell permeated the space. Tables and couches were strung around the room, and two cats slept on the window seat.

Sid stepped carefully around the tables to avoid knocking off the chairs that were stacked on top of them. Someone said, "We're closed."

The voice came from behind the bar. A young woman stood in the shadows. Her purple hair hung past her shoulders. She had a ring in one of her eyebrows and another in her painted black lip.

"I'm sorry, but I'm actually here about the job," Sid said.

She came to the front of the bar and sat on the counter. She wore a black T-shirt with the letters "AC/DC" on it and short shorts with ripped tights.

"You new around here? I thought I knew all the kids in town."

"Yes, my family and I moved here about a week ago."

"Where do you live?" she asked, popping her gum.

"Down on Shelby Street." The lone house on Shelby spooked most of the local residents, or at least that's what Theo said.

She snorted. "Yeah right, in the haunted house. Like I haven't heard that one before."

"I don't know about haunted, but my family owns the home, and we moved back in."

"Explain to me why someone whose 'family' owns King's Castle needs money."

"My parents feel I need to learn how to work a real job."

"Huh," she paused, twirling her hair. "No."

"Why not?"

"You'll need to find a 'learning experience' somewhere else." She jumped off the counter and went back to the sink.

"That doesn't explain why." Sid followed her, hoping to understand her immediate rejection of his possible abilities. He didn't feel anger coming from her. On the contrary, she was attracted to him.

She turned to face him, her shoes squeaking on the hardwood floor. Sid stood only a few inches from her. She inhaled and squeezed her eyes shut. He backed away, realizing he may have overstepped his bounds a little.

"Because you obviously have no previous work experience, and as soon as it gets busy, you're gonna quit. You've no incentive to keep the job. Offer me one good reason why you'll still be here in November, and I'll consider it."

Sid thought about everything Theo taught him over the last week. "My parents told me if I don't get, and keep, a job, they will take away my car."

"Humph," she said, smiling. "What do you know about coffee?"

"Absolutely nothing except that it has a distinct odor." She scowled at him and turned around again, wiping the counter. "But I'm an extremely fast learner. In one week I've learned how to use a computer, television, iPhone, Facebook, and Twitter."

"And why didn't you bother learning about those things before last week?"

"Because I didn't have them before last week."

She grinned, and Sid could tell she was about to give in.

"Where did you say you moved from?"

"I didn't."

She shook her head. "Never mind. I suppose we can try this for a week and see how you do. My summer help has all gone home, and Aspen isn't back from Hawaii yet." She handed him a piece of paper. "Call me Ella. Here's a list of all the drinks we serve and their ingredients. Have it memorized by tomorrow morning and wear sneakers. The floor has a tendency to get slick. Any questions?"

"Yeah. The name 'The Purple Dragon,' where did it come from?"

"Aspen," she said, pointing at a small picture next to the register. "She took that picture."

"Who took this picture?" Sid asked, walking toward it. In a crooked blue frame, the tips of pine trees lined the bottom of the picture and white clouds hung in the corners. Filling the middle of the picture was a violet dragon, Jolantha. Sid's mother's best friend.

"Aspen. Have you been paying attention to me?"

Sid looked at her. "What, oh yeah, but how'd she get it? Most people are terrified of dragons."

"Aspen is not most people"

"Can I meet her?" Sid asked, wondering if she could possibly be the girl he saw on the mountain in the park. Humans detested dragons. For there to be more than one person in the area who didn't run from them would be too much to ask. Plus, he hoped she was the same girl. He wanted to see her again.

"Yeah, she works here, but she won't be back in town until Saturday. She'll probably come to the party here Saturday night. Will you be going to the high school?"

"Yes. I'll be a senior."

"You should come. Most of the juniors and seniors will be here. I can introduce you."

He leaned closer to the picture. "Amazing. Does she take photos of dragons often?"

Ella cackled. "You're fighting a losing battle."

"I don't understand."

"I can already tell. You'll like her, but she won't like you."

"Why would she dislike me?" Sid asked, shocked.

"Oh, Aspen hates all the pretty boys. And you, my friend, are the very definition of a pretty boy. You look like you just pranced off the cover of GQ with your long black hair and smoldering eyes." She smirked at him, and he stood there, embarrassed for the first time in his life.

CHAPTER 6

A SPEN'S NIGHTMARE WALKED through the door of the Purple Dragon. It'd been three years since she saw the face that haunted her dreams. Marc should've never found her, yet there he stood, seemingly unsure of where to go. Stubble peppered his jaw, and thick eyebrows came together as he scanned the room. Bitterness crawled across her tongue.

The burgundy mug slipped from her hand and shattered; hot coffee seeped into her sandals. She ripped her eyes away from Marc. Dark brown liquid carved a path through the crevices and slid into the cracks of the faded wood floor. Breathe, she reminded herself. The smell of coffee beans and chocolate chip cookies filled her nostrils.

Brad glared at her from behind the espresso bar and reached for the broom and dustpan. Everything moved in slow motion. She looked toward the door, ready to face him again, but Marc was gone. Time sped up. She spun in circles, searching for him, praying he wasn't behind her. He had disappeared.

Was he really here? For a while his face had been a regular participant in that time between semi-consciousness and sleep. On those days, she pictured him everywhere. Except for the dream just before she left for Hawaii, she hadn't thought of him in nearly six months. She wondered if she saw him because of the dream.

She hated the fear consuming her. Aspen was the queen of everything dangerous. She played with bears, jumped out of airplanes, and chased after dragons. In third grade a boy at school dared her to jump off the top of the school—she broke her leg but won the dare. Nothing scared her, ever.

Except him.

"Aspen!" A squeal erupted in her ear. Tori hugged her from behind, and Aspen stiffened, still fearing what she couldn't see. Then Tori dragged her over to a table, and Aspen sat down, looking everywhere for Marc.

"Oh my gosh, I've missed you so much. At least you made it back in time for the party. It was so not cool that you disappeared on us for the last three weeks of summer. How was Hawaii? Lots of hot guys?" Her voiced squeaked a little, like it always did, sounding as if she were getting over a cold.

Tori paused for a moment, reached across the table, and grabbed Aspen's purse. She plucked out the Guava Lip Smackers. "Coty went home yesterday. I cried all night, and you were on a stinkin' airplane. I think I'm in love with him, but how can I love him in California? He promised to call and text and e-mail every day, but I bet one of those beach sluts takes advantage of him."

Coty showed up at the beginning of the summer. Tori knew he was only a summer fling. He probably already had a girlfriend in Cali, but it was Aspen's duty as BFF not to mention that. Besides, she felt woozy. Could she even stand?

Tori pulled out a box of mints and looked up at Aspen. "Are you feeling okay? You don't look so hot."

Duh. Of course she didn't look good. Control was her thing— nothing rattled her—this was a fluke. Aspen wondered if Tori could see her shaking. Tori put on Aspen's lip gloss and then tossed it into her own bag. If Aspen had been feeling normal, she would've been annoyed. Tori always took her things. Over the course of the last several months, she also changed her appearance so she looked more and more like Aspen. Her short red curls had morphed into straight blonde hair, except not as long as Aspen's. As it was, tonight, Aspen didn't care. This was one party she needed to ditch.

"Jet lag, I think."

"You need something to drink. But first, tell me about Hawaii. I heard you missed your flight."

"Who told you that?"

"Rowan. Normally I ignore his texts, but since you never had your phone on, he was the only way I had to keep tabs on you."

Aspen's brother and his big mouth. He'd say anything to impress Tori.

"Well, he exaggerated. We didn't miss our flight to Hawaii. Just the one out of Idaho Falls. We caught the next flight and still managed to make the connecting plane."

"How was it? What'd you do?"

"I got pictures of a fire dragon. Do you want to see them?" The red dragon hadn't gotten close to her like the black one, but Aspen still got good pictures.

Tori's face scrunched up, and she shivered. "No. And don't talk about them. They're creepy." "Then don't ask," Aspen snapped.

Tori pouted, and Aspen backtracked. "Tori, I'm sorry. I'm not feeling well. I think I should go home."

"But you just got here. Let's get something to drink, and you'll feel better." Tori gathered up her things, looped Aspen's purse over her shoulder, and pulled her off the stool. Aspen looked toward the door, just to double check Marc wasn't standing there anymore. Tori stopped, and Aspen ran into her.

"What are you doing?"

She grinned and pointed. "I think I found Coty's replacement."

Marc stood in the doorway by the stairs, next to the espresso bar. He turned his head, and for a moment, stared straight into Aspen's eyes. He gave her a crooked grin, and the acidic taste of bile rushed up her throat. She turned and threw up all over the floor.

"Eww. Oh eww." Tori's feet pranced on the ground. Louder footsteps approached, and a paper towel appeared in front of Aspen's face.

"Thanks," she mumbled.

Aspen held the paper towel over her mouth and stumbled toward the bathroom, Tori following. She sat on the counter while Aspen washed her face.

"You *are* sick," Tori said as they walked into the crowd. "I'm sorry I didn't believe you. Will you be able to make it home okay?"

"Yeah, of course." The crowd had gotten bigger, and the walls seemed closer together. The people pressed in on all sides, either ignoring Aspen or welcoming her back from Hawaii. She smiled, nodded, and forced her way to the front door, fighting both nausea and dizziness.

Seconds before she pushed the screen open, a hand grabbed her shoulder. She froze, unsure of what to do. Everything was so loud, the voices, the chairs scraping the floor, the bass of the music beating along with her heart. Aspen turned slowly and came face-to-face with her deepest fear.

All sound died. His lips moved but no words came out. Aspen's ears were deaf to the music and the screech of the coffee machine. The only thing she heard was the blood rushing in her ears.

Marc had a terrible, frightening, beautiful face. She noticed strange things—his one crooked tooth, the bare spot on his chin with no stubble, and the odd ocean-blue color of his eyes. Her vision blurred, and she swayed. Blue? Marc had brown eyes. His hand gripped her arm. Her eyes moved from his face to his hand that held on so tightly it almost hurt. Then her eyes rolled back in her head and everything went black.

"Aspen, wake up." Small hands slapped the side of her face.

"That's not going to work. Here, let me help," a deeper voice said, still female. Ammonia stung her nostrils, and her eyes opened. Ella's face hovered over Aspen.

"Good. See, she's fine."

Ella offered Aspen a hand, and she took it. Even unsteady on her feet, she surveyed those around her—Ella, Tori, Matt, and a couple of freshman she didn't know.

"Where's Marc?" Aspen asked.

"Who's Marc?" Tori asked.

"Never mind," Aspen said, grabbing her keys from the floor.

"Oh, no you don't." Ella took them from her. "I'm taking you home. You can get your car tomorrow."

Ella's Bronco sped down Highway 89. Aspen closed her eyes and let her mind wander. The last time she saw Marc, it was through her own swollen blackened eyes as he ran from her in the forests of Yosemite. She could still smell his sweat and the stink of alcohol on his breath.

People didn't come to Gardiner by accident, and they didn't just pass through. The town got enough tourists, but by the end of August most of them had gone home. Plus, they didn't come to the parties at the Purple Dragon unless someone local invited them. Did he come to find Aspen? She couldn't remember if she told him where she lived.

The face from the party floated in her head. In spite of what he did to her, she still found him attractive. Especially his eyes. Something about the thrilling deep blue color caused her face to flush.

"We have to go back," Aspen shouted.

"Calm down. We're a half-mile from your house. Whatever you forgot we can get tomorrow. You've already puked and passed out in my shop tonight, and I'm not taking you back."

"Please, I have to. I need to know."

"Know what?"

How could Aspen explain? She never told anyone about Marc, not even her parents. Ella wouldn't get it. Marc had brown eyes.

CHAPTER 7

ELLA EXPLAINED TO Aspen's parents that she threw up, fainted, and was hallucinating. Although, Aspen wasn't sure where she got that from. Aspen's mom, used to her brother's frequent bouts of anxiety, handed Aspen a bowl of ice cream. She ate it without thinking and realized, too late, that her mom spiked it with Valium. Unaccustomed to the medication, Aspen was out in fifteen minutes and didn't wake until Monday morning. Just in time to leave for school.

Tori pounced on her as soon as she entered the school.

"Oh my gosh, you missed an amazing party. There's this new guy. Oh man, so hot. His name is Sid, and he's going to be my new boyfriend."

Aspen smiled. "What about Coty?"

Tori gave her a dismissive wave. "Ancient history. He's in California, and Sid is here, available, and gorgeous."

Tori chattered on while they walked to homeroom. This was Aspen's last school year ever. If she passed. She'd rather be in the wild, doing something crazy. For the most part she tried, but only to keep her parents off her back. Somewhere along the line, rule number five came into play: graduate.

She didn't really see the point. After all, as soon as she was done, she was going to find a film crew that was as crazy as she was and head out in the parks to get close to the dragons. But Aspen wasn't dumb. She realized the possibility of making cash right away filming the dragons was low, and she needed a place to crash. As long as she kept her parents happy, she'd have a place to sleep. She'd graduate in the spring if it killed her. And it just might.

Mrs. Dufour had been her homeroom, and favorite, teacher for the last three years. They shared the same love of photography. Though Mrs. Dufour preferred to get shots of the wolves in the park instead of the dragons. This morning Mrs. Dufour focused her attention on a frazzled Lila, class president and probable valedictorian. Lila always had something to worry about, and since most of her peers didn't care, the teachers got to listen.

Aspen headed to her normal desk, back right corner. But sitting in her seat was Marc—or whatever his name was—fiddling with a pencil, his long hair shadowing his face. What the hell was he doing here? This guy was supposed to have been a one-night freak, a friend of someone at the party.

Graduation suddenly seemed so far away. No way would Aspen make it through the year if every time she turned around, he paralyzed her with fear. Time to drop out and tell Ella she wanted full time hours. She'd just have to work around her dream. Aspen spun and hurried out the door. Tori scurried after her.

"Aspen, what are you doing? I want to introduce you to Sid."

"Who's Sid?" Aspen asked, her head spinning.

"You know, the hottie from the party at the Purple Dragon. Were you not listening to me this morning? He hung out with us for most of the night. He's super sweet. You'll like him." She grabbed Aspen's hand and tried to drag her into the room. Aspen pulled away and leaned against the lockers in an effort to keep herself upright.

"What did you say his name was?"

"Sid," she said, crossing her arms and clicking her heels on the floor. "Are you sure?"

Tori sighed. "Of course I'm sure. I spent half the night with him. Don't you think he would've told me if I called him the wrong name? Now come on, he wants to meet you."

Aspen put her hands on her knees, leaned over, and took a couple of deep breaths. His name was Sid, not Marc. He was not the same person who destroyed her. But her throat was closing up, her brain was shutting down, and her mouth went dry.

"Why does he want to meet me?" Aspen whispered.

"He saw that picture in the PD that you took of the dragon. He couldn't stop talking about it." Tori grimaced.

No freaking way. Aspen couldn't even stand to look at him, and he wanted to meet her because of her dragons. How could he have such an effect on her? Aspen tried to remind herself of all the times she should've been scared but was not. Nothing came to her. Her head swam. Mr. Long Dark Hair made her feel like she was going to vomit. Fear was for little girls and psychotic brothers. Of which, Aspen was neither. She had to go in there and face him.

She stood upright and moved toward the door. Tori grabbed her arm.

"Listen, I really like this guy. Can you be nice to him?" Aspen nodded. That was one way to make sure he didn't hang around. Most guys who went out with Tori disappeared when the relationship was over because she was a little obsessive.

They walked in, and Aspen set her stuff on a desk in the front of the room, as far away from Sid as possible, even though that meant she couldn't hide from Mrs. Dufour. Tori pulled her to his desk.

"Sid, this is Aspen," she said and hurried across the room to say hi to Dan. This was new. Usually Tori would stay and hover. Aspen only saw her act like this once before, and that was a year ago when a celebrity came to spend a summer here. Aspen couldn't even remember his name, he wasn't that famous, but Tori was crushing on him bad. She barely said two words to him, but she talked *about* him all the freaking time.

"Hey." Aspen's voice was too soft, almost inaudible. Sid looked up, and she studied his face. Once again, his eyes captured her. They were the color of bluebirds—unnatural, but familiar somehow. Definitely not Marc's. Everything else, the long thick lashes, the dark skin, and the strong jaw—looked so similar. They still dug up all those old feelings of shame. Sid smiled. Aspen's knees buckled, and she sat in the desk in front of him.

Marc—no Sid—leaned across his desk. "How'd you get a picture of a dragon?"

"With a camera and a lot of patience." It was her standard answer. Most people had never seen a dragon because dragons avoid densely populated areas. They were protected, so people were not allowed to hunt or capture them. Not that it would do any good to try.

The national park system grew up around areas with large concentrations of dragons. Aspen was part of a very small group of people in the world who tried to find them. Most people feared them, though she had no idea why. Whenever she asked anyone, she got lots of "they're so big," or "they start forest fires," and her personal favorite, "I've heard they eat people." No one had ever shown an interest, except Sid—who made goose bumps rise on Aspen's arms.

He looked perplexed.

"I like dragons. I do a lot of hiking and backcountry camping. My camera is always ready," she explained.

"Do you have pictures of any others?"

Aspen didn't want to look at him and see that face. "Here," she said, handing him her phone. "These are the red ones I got last week."

She traced the edges of an old graffitied "John was here" on the desk, avoiding his gaze.

"This is unheard of," he said.

Aspen looked up. He was a mere eight inches from her face. His eyes locked on hers. Fear and desire burned in her stomach. Her lips tingled with the memory of her first kiss, the one Marc gave her three years ago. Would Sid's kiss taste different?

"Welcome back." Mrs. Dufour's voice jarred Aspen out of her trance, and her face flushed with embarrassment.

She slipped away and went to her own seat.

After homeroom, Mrs. Dufour called Aspen up to her desk. Tori followed.

"I wanted to show you some of the shots I got this summer."

Aspen thumbed through the pictures. She'd gotten some decent pictures of the wolves.

"They are nice. Did you get a new lens?"

"Yeah. You should know that your dragons were lower than normal when I was taking shots. You should join me next time."

"That'd be nice, let me know when you go."

Tori picked up one of the pictures and addressed Mrs. Dufour. "Maybe you can learn something from Aspen because her pictures are loads better than this."

Mrs. Dufour's face flushed, and Aspen dragged Tori out of the room.

"Why are you being so mean?"

"She gave me a D in English last year."

"Tori, that's because you lifted your final essay from the web. You're lucky she didn't fail you."

"Whatever. I don't like her."

Biology was boring as usual, but at least Sid wasn't in that class. Things were looking up. Most of the same kids who were in *biology for bimbos* were also in *math for morons,* so chances were he wouldn't be in Aspen's math class.

Tori met Aspen at their lockers.

"How's history?" Aspen asked.

"I have no idea. I slept," she replied.

"Was Sid in your class?"

"Nope. What'd you think about him?"

"He was nice."

"Yeah," Tori sighed. "Those eyes are to die for, aren't they?"

"That they are." Aspen grinned, hoping she was convincing.

Tori crossed her arms and glared at Aspen. "Hey, he's mine. You understand?"

"Defensive much? I'm not interested in him. I was just agreeing with you."

Tori moved her books from one arm to the other, and her blonde hair fell into her eyes. That was when Aspen noticed it.

"Did you get colored contacts?"

Tori looked up at her. "What? Oh yeah. Do you like them?"

They were the color of Aspen's eyes. What the hell was going on with her? The conversation shifted after that when several others walked up to them.

Aspen dawdled in the hallway, chatting with Tori and Matt, Aspen's puppy dog. He'd been after Aspen for most of her junior year. He was decent looking with tight curly brown hair and a nice build since was a swimmer. Near the end of the year, she agreed to go to prom with him. They had a good time, but relationships and Aspen didn't mix. Aspen deleted his texts and ignored his calls throughout the summer, but he was not to be deterred.

Matt looked at his watch. "We're going to be late, you coming?"

"Yeah, just give me a sec."

"I'll save you a seat."

Aspen nodded, opened her locker, and shoved in her biology book, knowing it would not come out again until the end of the year. The first day of school was the only day she used her locker, and that was just so she could store the books without losing them.

The hallways were empty. She was about to be late to math. Her favorite class, yippee. Maybe she should go home and avoid Sid that way. Or maybe she should go to math, which was the opposite direction of Dr. VanDyke, the principal, who knew of her habit of skipping out.

Aspen slipped into class one minute late. She was being stealthy, but Ms. Weber noticed anyway.

"Aspen, how nice of you to join us. If you'll take the desk in front of Mr. King, we can get started."

Sid sensed her panic as she slumped into the seat, took out a notebook and pen, and rested her chin on her hand without looking back. She had a knot on the back of her head with several sticks holding it in place. She emanated anger and hostility, so far the only person to feel that way around him. Which he found odd because she was the girl from the mountain. The one who felt excited to see a dragon, not scared. He couldn't wait to get to know her.

Ms. Weber droned on about equations. To Sid, school was pointless; he learned all this two hundred years ago. He wanted to talk to Aspen, to hear her voice, to understand her desire to chase the dragons.

Near the end of class, Ms. Weber finally stopped talking. Sid leaned forward to talk to Aspen, but Matt, who was sitting next to her, beat Sid to it.

"Have you heard anything about the missing climber?" Matt asked, pulling his chair to her desk.

"Why, was he staying at your place?"

"Yeah." Matt fidgeted with his pencil, and it broke in half.

"I wish I had more to tell you." Aspen frowned. "My parents weren't home when I left for school. Rowan said they'd been gone all night. Are the rest of the guests nervous?"

"Yeah, he was a college kid, and his parents are freaking out. It's always my folks' fault when they decide to do something stupid and fall off a cliff."

"I'll ask my mom or dad when I get home, but I gotta work after that."

"Great. I'll stop by and see you, get some of this homework done."

The teacher walked up to her as Matt slid his chair back to his own desk.

Ms. Weber sat on the edge of Aspen's desk. "You're a senior this year."

"I know."

"You're still in Algebra I."

"I know."

"If you don't pass my class, you don't graduate. And to pass my class, you must do your homework."

Aspen shoved her notebook into her bag. "Have I ever failed one of your tests?"

Mrs. Weber shook her head. "But you've never scored higher than a D+ either."

"Exactly. I sit here in your class every day, I pass my tests, and yet somehow I still fail. I don't do homework."

"If you want to graduate, you will."

The bell rang, and Aspen stalked out of class, angrier than when she arrived. At least Sid knew it wasn't just him she couldn't stand.

Still unsure of what to do after school, Sid drove over to the PD to talk to Ella. She was much easier to relate to than those he met at school, more at ease around him, not intimidated. Plus, she knew Aspen.

The old house was empty except for Ella. The smell of burnt coffee assaulted his nose. Would he ever get used to it? Ella wiped down the counter and threw her towel into the sink. She had her back to Sid, and her head bobbed up and down.

"Hey, Ella," Sid said, sneaking up behind her.

She jumped and yanked out her ear buds. "Sid, you scared me." She picked up a towel and flicked it at him.

"Sorry. Who's working tonight?"

"Aspen."

At the sound of her name Sid's heart raced. He tried to understand his need to know her. She was the only human he'd met (and there hadn't been many) who didn't detest dragons. That in itself made him curious, but she despised him. He'd given her no reason to.

"Who else?"

"Me. The idiot who was supposed to work with her called in sick."

"I'll work for you."

"Sid, that would be wonderful. I've been here all day." She rubbed her hand across her forehead, leaving a streak of coffee.

"Yeah, but you have to do me a favor," Sid said, handing her a clean towel.

"Sure thing."

"From here on out, you need to schedule Aspen and me together."

She grinned. "I told you you'd like her." Ella understood his fascination with Aspen, probably better than he understood it himself. He didn't understand his human feelings at all.

"That's still to be determined. She won't talk to me. At all. I figure if I'm working with her, she'll have to."

"Oh, don't underestimate her. I'm sure she could go through an entire shift without uttering a word."

Theo sat at Sid's desk, messing with the computer, and didn't acknowledge Sid's presence. The clock on the dresser said Sid had exactly thirty minutes to dress and get back to the shop. He didn't want to give Aspen any reason to be irritated with him.

"Find anything taboo on there?" Sid asked.

Theo took off his glasses and rubbed his eyes. "You know I have to do this. It's my job."

"No one else had people snooping through their stuff," Sid grumbled.

"Actually, you'd be surprised. But, Sid, you're no ordinary dragon. If I don't do this, the council will send someone else who is more thorough."

"I know, but I'm not going to do anything stupid."

"Says the dragon who broke the heart of Winerva's niece."

"I never gave Candide any reason to think I was interested in her. Why are you bringing that up? It happened over twenty years ago."

Theo chuckled. "I know. I'm just giving you a hard time. You working tonight?"

"Yeah."

"Will that Ella chick be there? If so, I'm going with you."

"No. I'm working with Aspen. How do you know Ella?"

"I scoped out the Purple Dragon today. She's hot. I guess I'll just have to wait until tomorrow."

Sid looked at the clock again, twenty minutes left. "Listen, Theo, I need your help with something, and I can't have you blabbing. Can you keep a secret?"

"What'd you do?"

"Nothing yet. The council won't approve, but I need your advice and master researching skills."

Theo leaned back on the chair and rested his bare feet on Sid's bed. "Why?"

Sid tossed him the *Your Human Years* book and grabbed his work clothes out of the closet.

"Turn to Chapter Five," Sid said, undressing.

"Chapter Five. Romantic Relationships." Theo snorted without opening the book. "Did you bother to read all the warnings before you read the tasks?"

"Yes, and I know what I'm doing."

"No, you don't." Theo put the book down and walked toward him. "You've only been at this for three weeks. You still don't understand human feelings. Chapter Five says do not try any of these until the sixth year for a reason. You'll be sealed before you've realized what happened."

"I was with Skye for a hundred and sixty-two years and managed not to get in trouble. I think I can handle a human girl."

"No, you can't." He paused for a minute. Then he lay on Sid's bed and spread his arms out, his expression far away. "I spent ten years living around them, and I was lucky I never got into trouble. Human girls are incredibly seductive. More so than any dragon I've ever met. They have ways of making you feel like you're on fire.

"I used to surf with a girl named Hazel. She had this smile to die for. We hung out for a summer, and I nearly gave up everything for her. She was the only human I kissed, and my lips still burn when I think about her."

Did he seal himself to her? Sid looked for the scrawled circle that marked the sealing, but saw nothing. Theo's eyes were closed, and a small stream flowed from the corners of his eyes. Sid looked away, embarrassed. Theo never talked about stuff like this. In fact, he never had a mate that Sid knew of. He was the good one, saving himself for the queen. Not that the rest of them did anything to jeopardize their chances for the kingship, but they played closer to the edge of the cliff than Theo. Sid was really the only one who nearly sealed himself to someone. He was good and he didn't, but there was a time with Skye that he thought about it.

Theo spoke again, his voice cracking, "I don't know how any of us make it through unscathed. You won't be able to resist. Plus, you know what will happen if you seal."

Sid pulled on his shirt and buttoned it up. There had to be a way to convince Theo he wouldn't let that happen. "This girl absolutely hates me. I'm not going to seal myself to her. I just want to get to know her. When I do, I'll be able to cross several things off that stupid list, which gets me closer to going home. If I finish in less than ten years, they'll let me be done." Looking in the mirror, Sid pulled his hair back. He liked it better when it hung down, but Ella said if she found a long black hair in the coffee, he would be fired. The clock read ten to four.

"I have to go," Sid said. "While I'm gone, find out everything you can about Aspen Winters and her family."

CHAPTER 8

ASPEN GOT TO work a half hour early in the hope that someone would do her homework for her. The math book somehow found its way into her backpack. Throughout her entire high school career, not one book had ever made it past her locker, and she managed to pass all her classes. Except math. Mrs. Weber made it very clear that if graduation was to happen, then she had to do her homework. Ugh.

Ella brought Aspen a latte.

"Homework? You?" Ella had on her Guns and Roses outfit today. *November Rain* played in the background. Aspen was more of an alternative rock fan, but she still appreciated Ella's taste in music.

"I think they're trying to kill me this year. You wanna do this for me?"

"Hon, I barely passed the first time. What makes you think I'd be able to help you with that?"

Aspen shrugged and looked at her book, the numbers and letters swirling together.

"Who's working with me tonight anyway?"

"The new guy."

Aspen groaned. She'd be better off alone.

"Ella, you know I hate training."

"You won't have to train him. He worked with me all last week while you were off playing in Hawaii, and he's a fast learner. Give him two weeks, and he'll be up to speed. In the meantime, be patient with him." Ella crossed her arms and narrowed her eyes.

"Fine," Aspen said and looked at her homework. What was she supposed to do with all the Xes? Whoever put letters in math was crazy. Besides, all Aspen could focus on in class was the fact that the scary boy sat behind her. She found it odd that her mind could accept he wasn't Marc, but her emotions couldn't.

Ella sat across from Aspen. "Hey, do you mind punching in a few minutes early? I'd like to get going. You can do your homework on the clock if you want."

"Sure, what's up?"

"Nothing." Ella stood and went behind the counter before Aspen could ask her more questions.

Aspen gathered her books and headed to the back room. Ella put on her leather jacket. She didn't say anything to Aspen.

"You okay?" Aspen asked.

"Yeah, I'm fine. I'll see you later."

Why did she want to leave so quickly? Aspen stared out the window as Ella walked to her car. A young man in a white button down shirt walked up to her. New boyfriend, maybe. He enveloped her in a big hug, and Ella smiled wide. Aspen watched, happy to have something to tease her about tomorrow.

Ella tugged at his black ponytail and laughed. Then he turned and walked toward the shop while she drove away in her Bronco. He was soon out of Aspen's sight, and she went around the counter and stocked the teas so he wouldn't think she was snooping.

A voice behind her said, "Hey, Aspen."

Aspen whirled around. "What are you doing behind the counter? Only employees can be back here."

"I am an employee." Sid stood there with a stupid grin on his face.

"You're the new guy?" Aspen asked, her pulse racing.

"Yes," he replied, reaching around her to hang up his jacket. She closed her eyes, trying to make sense of the situation. He smelled of cedar and pine trees. If Aspen wasn't hyperaware that he was standing inches from her, she could've imagined herself in the middle of the forest.

"Unbelievable," she said to herself. "How did this happen to me?" She took deep breaths to calm her nerves.

He backed up. "This happens to be a good thing. I want to talk to you."

"Well, I don't have to talk to you. Sid, I don't mean to be rude or anything." Aspen wasn't sure he'd take a hint. She couldn't be friends with him. Ever. "Okay, yes, I do. I don't like you. I'm not going to like you, and we will never be friends. Let's get through the night, and then I can talk to Ella about the scheduling. Nothing personal, but this isn't gonna work."

"What's not going to work?"

"All of it, working together, hanging out, being study buddies. Whatever it is you want from me, you're not going to get it."

"I don't want anything from you. I just want to talk to you. Is that too much to ask?"

Aspen couldn't think of a response. The front door rattled, and Mrs. Little walked in. Aspen glared at Sid and went to the counter to ask what she wanted. Aspen wrote down the order and handed it to Sid. He looked at her for a moment then smiled that wicked smile of his.

"I don't know how to make a green tea latte. You'll have to show me."

He seriously underestimated her if he thought it would be that easy. No way would he win that fast. Aspen grabbed a cup and waved it in front of his face, then poured the milk into the steamer container and handed the milk to him, pointing to the steamer. He smiled again.

"Sorry, don't know how to use that either."

Aspen ground her teeth. Liar. If he'd been training with Ella, then he knew how to use the steamer. He probably knew how to make the whole thing. Aspen stuck the container underneath the steamer and pointed to the thermometer. Sid came and stood behind her. The movement startled her, and she dropped the milk. It splattered everywhere, soaking her slacks, and he had the nerve to laugh. Aspen resisted the urge to yell and shoved the mop into his hands. The other machine, although not meant to be used on slow nights, warmed up quickly, and she made the latte far from where Sid cleaned up the mess.

He kept his distance after Aspen handed Mrs. Little her latte. But he'd been waiting. When she accidentally looked at him, he spoke.

"I'm sorry I laughed at you. It's just that you're trying so hard to ignore me. Am I really that bad?"

Yes, Aspen thought. She looked past him and saw Wobbles sneaking around the corner. "Oh, no you don't," Aspen said and scooped him up. Wobbles was one of Ella's coffeehouse cats. He knew he wasn't allowed behind the counter, but that didn't stop him from trying eight times a day. Aspen put him on the window seat with his sister Wiggles. He meowed and nudged her hand, and Aspen petted him. Mrs. Little was reading a magazine, and a couple of kids from school were doing homework. The night would be long and slow. Might as well give math another shot.

A hole formed on the paper next to number thirty-four as she erased the problem for the third time. Sid sat across from her.

"You having trouble with those?" he asked. Aspen gave him what she hoped was a nasty look and tried reading the problem again. It was no use; she was never going to understand.

"Look," he said, pointing to the problem. "All you need to do is subtract seventeen from each side of the equal sign." Aspen handed him her pencil, and he demonstrated. If she talked to him, maybe she could convince him to do it for her. She was about to give up her vow of silence when Tori's voice rang out across the shop.

"I knew you'd be bored tonight. We've come to keep you company." Aspen was grateful for the distraction; with Tori there she didn't have to concentrate on ignoring Sid. Tori could do all Aspen's talking for her. Matt, Lila, and Dan followed her into the shop. Aspen rolled her eyes at Dan kissing Lila as soon as they cleared the door. They were the school sweethearts and had this stupid ritual that involved kissing every time they walked through a door together. It was nauseating.

Tori dropped her stuff on the table in front of Aspen. "You never texted me back. Where's your phone?"

Aspen shrugged.

"I swear, you must be the only person on Earth who doesn't have their phone attached to their hand."

Aspen used it, but she hated being stuck to technology. It didn't work in the woods anyway.

Before Tori could continue talking, Aspen turned to Matt, who sat next to her and flung his arm across the back of her chair. She moved her chair a few inches away from him, and he scowled but removed his arm. She smiled at him apologetically.

"I was going to call you later," Aspen said. Matt's eyes lit up, and she hoped he wouldn't be too disappointed in her reason.

"If she can find her phone, that is," Tori said.

Aspen rolled her eyes. She was certain her phone was in the pocket of her jeans that she wore to school. She just forgot to bring it to work.

"Anyway, I talked to my mom, and she said they found the climber's camera."

"Only the camera?"

"Not exactly, they also found a foot," Aspen said, grimacing.

"A foot? As in not attached to the body?" asked Matt.

"Exactly."

"How the heck do they find just a foot?" Tori asked, wrinkling her nose.

"No clue, bears are usually messier, and wolves don't leave anything. The foot was off by itself, no blood trail or anything."

"Did they see anything on the camera?"

"Nothing that suggested anything unusual. It looked like the last picture he took was in the middle of a cave. But there were no caves near the spot he was hiking."

"Aspen, you weren't supposed to tell anyone," Dan said. He shook his head and blew his shaggy hair out of his eyes. His parents worked at the park with Aspen's.

Aspen's mouth had no filter. Her mom hadn't exactly been talking to her this afternoon. She overheard her conversation with her dad. Although, Aspen didn't see the big deal.

"Who cares? People will know soon enough."

"No, they won't. My mom told me they're keeping the foot secret. The rangers don't know what they're dealing with, and telling everyone could create unnecessary panic."

"Oops."

"I bet it was a dragon. They wouldn't leave much behind," said Tori.

Aspen scowled at her. "Dragons don't eat people."

"How do you know?" Tori asked.

"It hasn't ever happened before. Why would they start eating people now?"

"They've been eating people forever. We don't hear about it because no one survives."

"Where the hell do you get your information?"

Tori scooted closer to Sid. "Everyone knows it, but no one dares to say it in front of the mighty Aspen. We've been waiting for proof. Maybe now you'll stop taking pictures of those creepy things."

Aspen burned with fury. Tori was her best friend, but in this instant she couldn't stand her.

"Aspen's right. They don't eat people," Sid spoke up from next to Tori. He had a busted pencil in his hand and her math book open in front of him. He looked concerned. Aspen handed him another pencil. Indecision was etched across Tori's face. Aspen almost laughed at her dilemma. Tomorrow Tori would be singing a different tune about dragons.

Matt got up. "Thanks. I should tell my folks and let them know to keep it quiet."

Tori turned to Aspen. "Can you get me something to drink? I'm parched."

"Sure, what do you want?"

"The usual," she replied.

"The usual? Tori you've been coming here for the last three years, and you never order the same thing."

Tori grabbed Sid's hands, and he jumped. "What do you think I should get?" He stared at her hands for a minute and then at Aspen with a perplexed look. He didn't realize Tori had it bad for him, and Aspen almost pitied him. He paused for a second then said, "A green tea latte."

"Oh, those are good. Can you make it for me?"

"Only if Aspen shows me how."

"Never mind, Tori. I got it."

He followed her anyway.

Aspen brought Tori her latte and left Sid behind the counter. A few minutes later Tori giggled. Aspen turned to see what she was looking at. Sid had both Wobbles and Wiggles up on the counter drinking milk from a bowl.

"Stupid freaking idiot," Aspen said, heading for the cats.

"Ah, you talked to me!"

Actually she didn't. She was talking to herself. Let him think what he wanted though. Aspen picked both cats up and moved them to the window seat.

Dan spoke up. "I think we should go. I need to tell my folks they'll need to do some damage control. We know Matt's parents won't keep it quiet."

"Sorry," Aspen mumbled.

"Tori, you coming?"

"Yep." She grabbed her bag, gave Aspen a hug, and kissed Sid on the cheek. His face reddened, and he went back to the table and continued scribbling on Aspen's math homework.

"I gotta use the little girl's room. Be right there," Tori said to Dan.

Dan waited until Tori was out of earshot.

"There's something else you should know."

Aspen snapped her head up. "What?"

"They strongly suspect it was a dragon. They can't prove anything, but you need to be careful."

"Are they reporting it as a dragon attack?"

Dan shook his head. "But if they can't figure out what it is, they might. Just to have an explanation. I know how much you love them."

Aspen bristled. They weren't dangerous, but if everyone thought they were eating people, everything would change. Right now, they were left alone. If word got out, it'd be a witch-hunt. Aspen had to prove they weren't dangerous. If she could just get close to one again, like she had with the black dragon, she could film him and show the whole world they weren't responsible for the deaths in the parks.

Aspen and Sid closed up in an almost easy silence. He didn't try to get her to talk to him again. Sid brought her coat and offered to help her put it on. Aspen hesitated, not wanting to give him the wrong idea, but then she slid her arms in the sleeves. It felt natural, almost normal. So did Sid walking her to her car. Aspen even let him open the door for her, but she didn't say anything to him.

"Here's your book. I did the assignment for you. You may want to copy it in your own handwriting." Aspen took the book and looked up at him in the darkness. He smiled and shut the door.

She drifted back three years to the memory of her first kiss. Marc had taken her to a movie and when they got ready to go home, he opened the car door for her. Before she got in, she looked up at him, and he smiled that same smile Sid had, bringing his face toward hers. She remembered feeling nervous because she'd never kissed anyone before. His kiss was soft like a gentle rain. Little did she know that gentle rain would turn into a major storm.

Aspen came back to the present and found herself alone in the parking lot. She turned on the radio and took out her math homework. Sure enough, it was done, but each answer had detailed instructions explaining exactly how to solve the problem. And short comments were written all over the page. Random things Sid thought she should know. "You should name your dragons. I like Valentine for the red one and Jolantha for the purple." "Wiggles and Wobbles don't like you much." "I wish you weren't afraid of me."

Okay, so he wasn't that bad. Sure, he was a tad annoying, but she probably presented him a huge challenge when she immediately gave him the cold shoulder. That was understandable. Challenges were meant to be attacked with no mercy. If the tables were turned, she'd be doing the exact same thing. It sucked to admit.

Why was Aspen backing down from him? She hadn't felt this kind of fear since, well, since she realized what Marc was going to do to her. She shivered. Maybe it was time for her to face this demon. Aspen wouldn't run from him. She wouldn't avoid him. She would attack this fear head on.

CHAPTER 9

S ID WENT STRAIGHT home after work, frustrated by Aspen's rejection. He had been unable to reach Theo on his phone to ask about his research on Aspen, so he raced up the stairs and stopped dead in his doorway. Seated on a chair next to Theo was Sid's sister, Pearl, the last person he wanted to see.

"You're angry," she said quietly as Sid dragged out his box of geodes, a newfound hobby, and sifted through them. "You shouldn't be. Just because I'm on the council doesn't mean I'm not on your side."

"Then why are you here?" Sid asked, digging under his bed for a hammer. "I thought I was allowed to have contact with my mentor, no one else."

"You're the king," said Theo sarcastically. "We've got to keep you safe. How am I supposed to do that without your sister?"

"Theo seems to believe you got in over your head. Anytime a dragon decides that they want to get romantically involved with a human, that's an issue. Especially within the first month. That's why I'm here. He thought perhaps I could talk some sense into you. So you tell me why I am here," said Pearl. She ran her fingers through her deep red hair. Pearl felt different somehow, a foreign emotion coming from her. She was usually solid and calm like the trees, but today she felt volatile like the ocean. Though she was radiating happiness and love. Sid forgot himself for a moment.

"You've been sealed," he said.

"Yeah." She grinned and stretched out her bare foot, revealing a thin golden script. The intricate pattern revealed no name.

"Who is it?" Sid asked, dejected. Blank etchings only meant one thing. Whoever she sealed herself to didn't love her back.

"Raja."

"And his name is missing because?"

"He wants to make sure you really become king before he allows himself to be sealed."

"That prick," Theo interjected. "Sid's gonna be king. Raja needs to give it up. Besides, he's been after you a long time. Why would he make you wait?"

She huffed and pulled her foot under her long silver skirt. "Raja's just being cautious. I can wait ten years. Plus, it's not exactly a conscious decision. He'll seal himself to me when he's ready. I love Raja. That's not going to change. Enough about me. We are here to talk about you, Sid."

"So, talk. I'm listening."

"Why am I here?" Pearl asked once again, exasperated.

"Did Theo tell you about Aspen?" Sid asked, turning over a geode in his hand, feeling the rough bumps to find its sweet spot. She nodded, and he continued. "I work with her. The first thing she said to me tonight was 'Sid, we're never going to be friends.' Then she didn't talk to me for the rest of the night."

"You mean like Winerva?" asked Pearl, her smile widening, and her eyes lighting up with laughter. "You do remember Winerva, don't you?"

"The evil white hag," Theo muttered. "That was the summer Skye tried to kill him," said Theo. "And poor Candide was heart—"

"Enough with my lousy love life," Sid said, pointing his hammer at them. "That has nothing to do with Aspen, and I'd rather forget about it. Find something else to gossip about."

Theo laughed, and Sid swung his hammer. With a loud *thunk*, the rock split exactly where he wanted, and showered Theo and Pearl with chalky dust and pea size chips; the inside revealed brilliant purple gems.

"Anyway," Pearl continued as though rocks had not rained down upon her. "It has everything to do with Aspen. Winerva hated you the moment she laid eyes on you." She reached down and snatched half of his rock. "You couldn't stand it. Obsidian must be liked by every-one," she said rolling her eyes. "Was there anything you did that sum-mer that didn't piss her off?"

"No," Sid said, picking up another rock and setting it down. With-out searching for a good spot, he swung the hammer again, and this time the rock shattered with a loud crack. Theo ducked as a shard flew past his head and splintered the computer screen.

"Watch it, will ya?"

Sid sighed. "Look, it's been a long day. Can you guys leave me alone for a little while?" He dug through the box again.

"No, I'm only going to be here for a week or so, and then I won't see my baby brother for the next ten years. I'm not going to leave you alone," Pearl said and sat on the floor next to him.

"You're not supposed to be here now, yet here you are."

Pearl laughed. "You're in a mood, aren't you? Maybe you're right, and I'll be back, but only if there's trouble, so let's hope I don't come back. Since I'm here, you might as well enjoy my company."

"Why are you only staying a week?" Sid asked, holding his hammer high above another geode.

"I have to start the search for the queen," she said.

Sid missed this rock entirely and put a hole in his floor. The search was starting early. The queen was the reason he never sealed himself to Skye. He knew Pearl would head up the search because she was the representative for the royal tribe, but he would know nothing of the queen until the council presented her before him for the testing.

Sid gave up on the rocks. "Why are you starting the search already?"

"It's always this early. We need a few years to narrow the field, and then they have to go through extensive training before the testing."

Sid shivered, thinking of the horror stories he'd heard about the testing. He'd never witnessed it, but only about half of the potential queens made it out alive. Even fewer made it out sane. Most kings had to watch three or four candidates go through the testing before one was finally accepted. Again, that choice would not be his.

"I talked to Skye," said Pearl, interrupting Sid's thoughts.

His stomach knotted. Of course she talked to Skye. Was there any part of his life his sister didn't stick her snout into? Sid waited, knowing that no matter what he said, Pearl would find away to get her point across.

Pearl continued. "She wanted me to tell you she is sorry for the way she left things."

Sid missed Skye. He'd give anything to have her sitting in front of him instead of Pearl. She had been the bright spot in his life, the one who made sure he always faced the sun instead of the clouds. Humanity would be more fun with her around.

"Where is she?"

"Back home in the Everglades. She stopped to see me on the way."

"Can I see her?"

"No, you know—"

"Would you like to know what I found out about Aspen?" Theo interrupted.

"Absolutely," Sid said as Pearl started to protest. Anything to escape the painful road his conversation with Pearl was heading. He picked up a shard of the shattered geode and ran his fingers across the tiny purple spikes.

"Almost every bit of information I found on her was attached to dragons. Did you know she has pictures of us?"

"Yeah, she showed me some this morning." Sid dug into his pocket, remembering he still had her phone. He handed it to Theo.

Theo thumbed through the pictures as Pearl watched over his shoulder.

"She actually likes dragons," commented Pearl, perplexed. "That's a bit, um, unusual."

"So why do you think she hates me as a human if she likes dragons?"

"Well, she doesn't know you're a dragon," said Pearl, taking the phone from Theo.

"She's going to hate you even more when she finds out you jacked her phone," said Theo, spinning around to the computer.

"I didn't mean to steal it. She ran off before I could give it to her, and then I forgot about it. I'll give it back tomorrow."

Theo scowled and pulled off a piece of the shattered computer screen. "You're going to have to replace this, you know. I wanted to show you the rest of the pictures she's taken, but that will have to wait. Anyway, Stacey and Jason Winters, her parents, are park rangers. As a child, Aspen moved from one park to another. My guess is that's where her fascination with dragons comes from; she's lived near us her entire life. The info on her family is sketchy. It looks like she has an older sister and a twin brother. They lead a quiet life."

Sid sighed, disappointed in Theo's research. *They lead a quiet life.* He thought Theo had better resources than that.

"Aspen, however, is almost famous," said Theo.

"What do you mean?" Sid asked.

"She's a bit of a daredevil," he said. "Aspen has two blogs. One with all her dragon pictures and one with the rest of her adventures. She skydives, hangs from ropes in the treetops, and has a black belt in aikido. Dude, she even swallows fire." Theo sounded impressed.

"So? We breathe fire," Pearl said.

"Yeah, but we're dragons."

CHAPTER 10

T HE NEXT DAY, Rowan got all snappy with Aspen because she made him ten minutes late to school. But no way was she giving Sid the opportunity to talk to her. She raced to biology and walked to math two minutes late. To her surprise though, Mrs. Weber and Sid were standing outside of the classroom talking.

"Sid, it is highly unusual for a senior to be in Algebra I. Where were you placed in your previous school?"

"I was homeschooled."

"I thought so. I'd like you to take a placement test today, just to make sure you're in the right class. I'd hate for you to be bored."

Sid nodded and caught Aspen's eye. He smiled, and her heart raced. She couldn't tell if it was because she was scared of him or attracted to him. Damn her feelings.

"What happens if I do well?" Sid asked.

"Then we'll move you into Geometry or Algebra II."

Sid moved to step around Mrs. Weber when she stopped him. "The library is that way," she said, pointing the opposite direction.

"Oh, right." He nodded to Aspen and turned.

Aspen tried to sneak past Mrs. Weber, but she was too observant. "You're late, Miss Winters."

"I know, but I did my homework."

Mrs. Weber raised her eyebrows. "Well, miracles do exist."

She disappeared into the classroom, and Aspen noticed that Sid still hadn't turned the corner.

"Hey, King," Aspen called.

"Yeah?" The eagerness in his voice betrayed his calm expression.

"Do your best on that test." Anything to get him out of that class.

"Not a chance. I'm going to miss all of them. Just for you." He grinned and disappeared around the corner.

He still hadn't come back by the time the bell rang. Which rocked. She ate lunch in the abandoned janitor's closet, and he wasn't in any of her afternoon classes.

At her locker that afternoon, while she was getting her stupid math book again, Tori stopped to talk to her.

"Why weren't you at lunch?"

"Detention," Aspen lied.

Tori nodded. That was a common enough occurrence she didn't suspect anything unusual. She leaned against the locker next to Aspen's and sighed.

"Sid sat with us. He's so sweet. Is it possible to fall in love without even kissing?"

Aspen held back her snort. "I don't think so."

"Well, I think so. I don't want to screw this up. What do you think I should do?"

"Are you really asking me for advice? I haven't dated anyone here."

"You went to prom with Matt."

"Only because you wanted me to. I don't like Matt."

"But he loves you, and he's not the first guy to fall in love with you. How do you do it?"

"Tori, I don't know. It's not like I want Matt falling for me."

"You're right. It's just you. I'm so jealous, but whatever. I'm going to get Sid if it's the last thing I do. I need to find something in common with him. But all he talks about is stupid dragons."

Aspen rolled her eyes. "There. You can use that. Just pretend to like them. Hello, you have me. I know more about dragons than anyone else."

Tori's eyes lit up. "I could do that."

"Look, I gotta go, or Rowan's going to have a panic attack wondering where I am. Why don't you come over for family game night, and we'll talk dragons and see how much we can say before Rowan pees his pants."

She laughed. "That's not very nice."

"That's the point. See you about seven?"

Tori nodded. "I gotta go find Lila. See you later." She gave Aspen a hug and disappeared into the crowded hallway.

Aspen tried to escape to the parking lot, but Sid caught her just before she went through the doors.

"You left your phone with me yesterday. I'm sorry. I forgot I had it."

"Thanks," Aspen muttered. Tori would be pleased she could finally answer her million and one texts.

"Wait," Sid said.

Jeez, what now? Aspen hesitated for a half second and pushed the door open. Whatever he had to say wasn't important enough for her to hang around.

"Aspen, wait," he yelled. All the freshmen waiting for their parents stopped mid-conversation.

"What?" Aspen kept her voice deliberately low and irritated.

He stared at her without speaking, those gorgeous eyes boring into hers. If she concentrated on them, she could forget he looked like Marc. Though, then she might do something stupid like kiss him because his eyes mesmerized her. She squeezed her eyes shut for a second to clear her head. Then she looked at him again with her eyebrows raised to let him know she was waiting. He didn't utter a word. Aspen rolled her eyes and made her way down the stairs.

"Dragons," he said, following her. "I know where you can find dragons."

Damn. That might be worth a conversation. Especially now. She had to prove they weren't dangerous before the public started suspecting them for the all of the deaths in the national parks.

"Where?" Aspen asked when they reached the bottom of the stairs. She couldn't look at his face so she studied his tennis shoes.

"Inside Yellowstone. Can I show you?"

Dragons. Sid. Dragons. Sid. His shoes were the expensive Adidas. Black with white stripes. She tried to avoid focusing on her sweaty palms and the anxiety filling her chest. Sid could show her where to find dragons, but that would mean she'd have to go somewhere with him. Alone. This was ridiculous. If anyone else on the planet had offered, she would have had her ass in the passenger seat already. Even if they looked like Marilyn Manson.

"Sure," Aspen said. "But first I need to drop my brother off at home. Follow me."

On the way to her house, she thought of a gazillion different ways to lose him. But the prospect of finding more dragons was too good to pass up. He'd only been in Gardiner for a few weeks, so how could he possibly have found a place she didn't know about? If he was lying, she'd finally have an excuse to use her aikido training.

In the house, she grabbed a couple of water bottles and granola bars. If Sid showed her the dragons, she had every intention of stalking them tonight. Her camera made it into her bag last.

Aspen climbed into Sid's black Escalade and buckled her seatbelt in silence. The inside of his car smelled warm and earthy like a cedar chest. They drove around the bottom loop and past Dunraven Pass. Aspen kept her gaze out the window and crossed her arms.

The silence was menacing. Words would not form in Sid's head to speak to her, and she certainly wasn't speaking to him. The scenery seemed to captivate her as they drove, though he was sure it was as familiar to her as it was to him.

Sid parked in a small gravel lot at the head of a trail.

"We are going to have to walk a bit. I hope that's okay."

She nodded and dug in her backpack. He hadn't noticed she brought it. She pulled out two bottles of water and handed him one.

"Thanks. We'll need to follow the trail until we run out of trees."

"I've been down this trail before. The tree line ends after about fifty yards."

Aspen disappeared into the thick of trees, and Sid chased after her. The trail sloped down, and the pines towered over them, providing him a view of trees he'd never seen before. The area was familiar, but it looked different.

From above, the individual branches weren't visible; the view was of a tree as a whole. From below, the details of the trees made them beautiful. Aspen hiked only a few feet in front of Sid, but never looked back. She was wound tight, and Sid had difficulty pushing her anxiety away. He had to breathe deeply to keep his chest from constricting. Pine needles crunched underfoot, offering the only sound in the silent forest.

Sid contemplated several ways to break the silence, but each seemed forced. No one had ever rendered him speechless before. It was maddening. No coherent thoughts entered his head, and he was surprised when Aspen spoke first.

"Tori would be furious if she knew I was here with you."

"Why?"

"She's madly in love with you. Surely even you can see that. And me, being here alone with you, she'd see that as her best friend encroaching on her territory." Aspen talked without looking back, her braid swinging from side to side. She laughed, her anxiety easing a little.

"Is that why you don't like me? Because you don't want to offend Tori?"

"No, I have other reasons for not liking you. But really, I think you should give Tori a chance. She's a little flighty, but sweet."

Her voice was soft but pierced the forest. Sid savored the sound of the words, but as happy as he was that she spoke, he didn't want to talk about Tori. He took a chance.

"Why are you so fascinated with dragons?" he asked, running his fingers along the bark of the trees.

Aspen turned around and walked backwards a few steps. She studied Sid's face for a moment. Her gaze held his for only a few a seconds, but in those seconds the forest seemed to still. The energy passing between them was unlike anything he'd felt before. Sid stumbled, and the spell was broken. When he found his feet again, she had disappeared down a hill.

When Sid caught up again, she spoke.

"Aside from humans, dragons are the only intelligent species on Earth," she said.

Her emotions shifted. Aspen began the walk hissing, and now she almost purred.

"What makes you think that?" Sid asked.

"They have intelligent thoughts. They're not like other animals. A dog can understand that an action is bad if he is taught, but ultimately he is driven by instinct. Humans and dragons think on their own. Instinct, to both dragons and humans, is a second nature, not first." She spoke without once turning to check if Sid was listening.

"How do you know?" he asked.

"Have you ever heard of a dragon attacking a human?"

"No." Sid tried to walk next to her, but she moved faster, crossing her arms and keeping her eyes on the ground in front of her, the claws coming out again.

"It is statistically impossible for it to have never happened. But I've researched every possible dragon attack. Not one was legit. If dragons were like any other animal, they would prey on humans. They are carnivores—we are meat."

"What if they don't like the taste of humans? Or what if documented reports don't exist because there are no survivors?"

"I suppose that's possible, but I don't believe it." She relaxed a little. Sid couldn't understand her mood fluctuations. If she was talking about the dragons, she was content, almost happy. If she sensed his presence, she felt angry and scared. He couldn't keep up.

"Why?"

"Sid, I'm only talking to you because none of my friends like hearing about dragons. You're the first person to have ever asked." She stopped and took a drink from her water bottle, glanced at him, and then looked away. "I'm going to call a truce today, but don't expect it to last. I'll go back to hating you tomorrow."

"Fair enough," Sid said, although he hoped the truce would last longer. Surely, she wouldn't change her mind again tomorrow.

"Can I tell you a story?"

"Sure." She could tell him a thousand stories as long as she kept talking.

"When I was four, I lived in the Everglades. My favorite place to be was on the water. My parents took me out at least once a day to search for alligators. One night, they got busy, and by the time dinner was over, my bedtime arrived. My mom put me to bed in spite of my kicking and screaming. After I calmed down, I climbed out of my window, hopped into a canoe, and floated into the bay.

"The first half hour or so was fun, but then I wanted to go home. I didn't know where I was and had no way to get back, and there was no oar. I leaned over the edge to paddle with my hands and fell in. I screamed and flailed and watched with horror as an alligator raced in the water toward me. I'll never forget that moment.

"Then, I felt the water drop away, and I was flying. I looked up and saw I was in the claws of a dragon. She landed at the edge of my driveway and put me down. I saw her clearly in the light of the full moon. She was gorgeous, silvery blue with sapphire eyes. Then she flew away."

Skye. Sid remembered that day. She came home the next morning all concerned she had done the wrong thing. She was afraid she hurt the little girl.

"An animal wouldn't have done that," Aspen continued. "An animal would have let me drown. Or eaten me. A being with intelligent thought recognizes the need to save another. That's why I'm not afraid of dragons. I fell in love that day. Dragons have a place in my heart that no boy could ever fill."

"Just like that?"

"Yeah, in fact the next night I took a permanent marker to my pink My Little Pony pajamas. From that moment on they had wings and fire."

Sid laughed, picturing a four-year-old Aspen. He was shocked at how much she knew about dragons. She was right about all of it. They didn't eat people. In general, they didn't prey on predators. Deer, elk, buffalo, and cows were their main food sources. Humans would be the last creatures on which they would feast. They thought intelligently, and over the years the dragons had formed an uneasy truce with humans. Since they are able to take a human form, it would feel cannibalistic to eat one.

"Have you managed to get close to a dragon since then?" Sid asked.

"Only once, about a month ago. I went rock climbing, and this huge black dragon landed on a cliff next to me. He was the most beautiful thing I'd ever seen. I keep going to the same spot hoping he'll be there, but I haven't seen him since."

"Good thing you are on this walk with me then, huh?"

"Why's that?"

"Because I'm going to show you how to find that black dragon again."

CHAPTER 11

MATT SUMMERS NEEDED to get away from things for a bit. His folks were on his case about school, and the girl he'd been after for the better part of two years was off with the new guy. He punched the steering wheel.

That guy was trouble. Aspen was the type to run off with a bad boy since she was an adrenaline junky. But Matt had his hopes.

The park was good for thinking. It was one of a few spots he liked to go and just sit. He wasn't a hiker, but the animals were nice to watch. As he drove around Dunraven Pass, he spotted Sid's SUV.

Prick.

He hadn't wasted anytime getting Aspen alone. Matt pulled over behind the Escalade. If Sid was putting the moves on Aspen and she didn't want them, then Matt could take her home. Then maybe she'd realize he was better for her than that asshole.

Matt grabbed his backpack and stepped out of the car. He didn't plan on hiking, but if Aspen and Sid caught him, he wanted it to look like he was out there for something other than to spy on them. He peeked into the windows of the SUV and saw nothing. They must've hiked down the trail. Matt leaned against the car door and pondered his next step. Walking down the trail seemed like a stupid idea. If Aspen really wanted to be alone with Sid, then he'd look like a desperate loser. On the other hand, if Sid was giving her attention she didn't want, Matt would be a knight in shining armor.

He knew if he walked out into the field, he could see the end of the trail with the binoculars in his bag and see if they were out there.

Matt traipsed into the middle of the field, set his backpack down, and rummaged for the binoculars.

He heard a rumbling above like thunder. He looked up, not sure what he'd see since the sky had been cloudless when he headed out. The golden underbelly of a dragon whooshed over top of him. His stomach knotted, and he bit back a scream. If he was so inclined, he could reach up and touch it. Though that was the last thing he wanted to do. Instead, he scrambled backwards without taking his eyes off it.

The dragon landed, and the ground shook, like a small earthquake. Matt fell over and froze, staring at the gigantic golden head heading straight for him. He didn't want to see his last moment, so he squeezed his eyes shut. The heat from the dragon's breath was unbearable, but it didn't last long.

The dragon knew he was getting careless. He hadn't meant to land, but he was so focused on his meal that he wasn't paying attention to his actions. This would get him into trouble someday, but part of him didn't care. He'd tasted human flesh, and now nothing else would suffice.

CHAPTER 12

S ID AND ASPEN finally reached the end of the trail where the trees gave way to an enormous grassy plain. Lazy buffalo grazed on the yellowed field. At the edge of the grass, a mountain range began, starting with smaller hills and rolling into vast peaks.

Sid stepped out from the trees behind Aspen and pointed to a small hill separating the field from the mountains. The heads of every single animal snapped up, and several birds, mostly eagles and hawks, settled in the trees directly behind them.

"See that hill over there?" he asked.

Aspen followed his finger. "You mean the one with the two trees?"

"Yes, that one. Every time I come here at dusk, a dragon lands there and drinks from the pond on the other side of the trees. If you ever want to get close to that dragon, I'd say that would be your best bet."

"How often have you seen them?"

"A few times. I don't come out here that often."

"Thank you," Aspen said, genuinely glad he brought her here. But her insides were starting to protest the close proximity. "We should go back," she said.

"Of course."

On the way to the road, Aspen thought about what he told her. He couldn't have been here longer than a month or two.

"You know, I've lived here for years and never found a spot where dragons land regularly, and I've been actively searching. How is that you just happened to find one?"

She turned to see his reaction. He just shrugged. "I like hiking and finding new trails. Yellowstone is one of best parks in the world. A few days after we arrived, I wanted to get out and explore. I found this trailhead and got lucky. I like dragons, and so I came back a few days later to see if I could spot him again. Sure enough, there he was. I've probably been out here four or five times since then, and he's always been there. Though I'm not quite as crazy as you. I didn't actually try to get close to him. You'll need to be careful."

Aspen grinned, and before she could stop herself, she asked, "Do you want to come with me?"

Sid froze. He looked like he wasn't sure what to say. "Thanks for the offer, but I think I'll pass."

Aspen was confused. He'd been chasing after her, and the second she mentioned spending time with him, he bailed. Maybe he was one of those guys who just liked the chase. Poor Tori. She didn't stand a chance.

Back at the gravel lot, Sid's car was not alone. Matt's car was parked behind him.

"I wonder what he's doing here," Aspen said.

They walked around Matt's car, but didn't see him. "Maybe he hiked a different trail," Sid suggested.

"There's no other trailhead. And Matt's not the type to go wandering in the woods." He must've stopped because he recognized Sid's car. Did he see her leave with Sid and follow them? He had a crush on her, but that would be creepy. Aspen looked out into the field and spotted a blue bag of some kind. "Do you see that out there?" she asked, pointing to the blue lump.

"Yeah, what do you think that is?"

"It looks like a backpack." She walked toward it, and Sid followed. As they got closer to the blue spot, the field was torn up like it'd been plowed.

The blue spot was definitely a backpack, or what was left of it anyway. It looked like Matt's. Aspen found the piece that had the Jansport logo. Most of the backpack was scattered in the field. She picked up some of the smaller pieces, and Sid went over to the biggest piece. She heard him gasp and turned to see him fall to his knees.

Aspen ran to him. "Sid, are you okay?" she asked, kneeling down next to him.

He pushed her away and jumped up. His face paled, and he spun in circles as if he were looking for something.

"Get away from there," he yelled, pulling on her arms. She'd been so busy worrying about him that she'd forgotten why they were in the field. She looked down where Sid had knelt. There on the ground was a freckled, severed arm.

Matt's arm.

CHAPTER 13

T HE STENCH OF blood was burned into Sid's nostrils. He
rolled his windows down and allowed the cold night air to
rush into his car, hoping to rid himself of the smell. He raced
through the forest toward home, away from Matt's arm, away from
the sirens, past blurred trees. Matt was dead. He was only seventeen,
a child. When Sid died, it would be on purpose and hundreds of
years from now. Matt had no choice, no way to defend himself from
the mouth of the monster that had killed him. He would never come
back.

Sid desperately wanted to forget what he'd seen. Instead, his mind
kept rolling through the scene. The arm, the broken pack, the distinct smell of sulfur, the deafening silence as he fell to the ground.
And the strange footprints. Footprints only he would notice and recognize. Footprints of a dragon. Humans saw them occasionally but
didn't realize what they were. They tore up the land, but they didn't
look like footprints.

Sid flung his car up the driveway and slammed on his brakes in front of his home, spraying gravel in the flowerbeds. Not a single light in the house was on. He flew up the stairs and into Theo's room, flipping on the lights. The bed was neatly made up. He listened to the house breathing, the quiet hum of the air conditioner, the tick of the branches hitting the window.

A scream interrupted the quiet house. Sid raced down the stairs and paused, unsure of which direction to turn. Curse this gigantic house. A woman screamed again, this time to his right, and began yelling incomprehensible words.

Sid tore off through the library, past the Picasso his mother had bought, and into the east wing. His heart beat furiously as he tried to think of why someone would be screaming in his home.

His footsteps echoed through the hall as he leapt up the short stairway. He stopped abruptly at the entrance to the movie room. On the wall on the far side, a masked man waved a machete at a woman. The woman turned to run, and the man grabbed her by her hair. Pearl squealed from the couch.

Sid bent over, breathing hard, his heart slowing. In front of him, Theo and Pearl were sitting on opposite ends of the couch. Sid crept up behind them and rested his hands on the cool leather.

"We need to talk," he announced.

Pearl jumped again, this time spilling popcorn over her lap. "Geesh, Sid, don't do that. Come, sit down. It's a great movie."

"We need to talk," he repeated.

"About what?" Theo asked, shoveling a handful of popcorn in his mouth, not taking his eyes off the screen.

"After the hike today—"

The woman on the movie screeched again, and Pearl covered her eyes. Sid was getting nowhere with the movie on. He grabbed the remote and pushed the pause button just at the man plunged the knife into the woman's heart, bathing the wall in a gruesome red.

"Hey," Theo attempted to wrestle the remote back.

Sid held the remote high above his head. "Look, I need to talk to you. You can go back to the movie in a sec. Will you just listen?"

"Fine."

"A friend of mine was killed today." Sid searched for the right words to express what he'd seen.

"Oh, Sid, I'm so sorry. What happened?" Pearl put down the popcorn and turned to face him.

Theo rolled his eyes. "Okay, can we get back to the movie now?"

Pearl glared at him. "Seriously, Theo, this is the first human he has known that died. Have a little more patience."

Sid rubbed his sweating palms on his jeans. He still couldn't believe a dragon had done this. Pearl brushed her hair away from her eyes.

"Go on, Sid. Tell us what happened." Pearl grabbed his hand and stared at him like an overly concerned mother.

Sid wasn't sure if anything could convey what had happened. Nothing brilliant appeared in his head, so he simply stated the facts.

"He was eaten by a dragon."

Pearl pulled her hand out of his and looked away. Sid waited for a response, knowing it wouldn't be a good one.

"Did you actually see who ate him?" Pearl spoke slowly, as if speaking to child.

"No, I didn't see the dragon." Sid paced in front of them.

"Because there wasn't one." Theo snorted. He picked up the bowl of popcorn again and ate, anger pouring off him.

Pearl's emotions were indifferent as her ice-blue eyes shifted back and forth between Sid and Theo.

"What makes you think it was dragon?" she asked.

"The only part of Matt we could find was his arm, surrounded by dragon footprints."

Pearl rubbed her eyes. "Impossible, we don't eat people."

"I know," Sid said. He sat on the floor and dug his fingers into the carpet. "But, Pearl, I know what I saw. It couldn't have been anything else. What are we going to do?"

Pearl didn't move. Theo continued eating and didn't bother to look at either of them. Sid waited, hoping Pearl's answer was the right one, or he was about to break a few rules and take care of it himself. Pearl finally spoke.

"*You* aren't going to do anything. I'll deal with it." She stood and her brilliant red hair flowed behind her as she swept from the room. He chased after her and found her in the driveway, her back to him.

Her transformation took seconds. Her hair disappeared, and her neck elongated. Fingers became gigantic claws, and a tail sprouted from her back. Sid blinked, and she looked normal. His own skin itched; he wanted to join her. His human form was too confining and weak. He couldn't do anything like this and wanted to be out there helping Pearl find this monster.

"I should come with you."

She faced him. *No, you are not allowed to become a dragon right now. You know that.*

Sid hated that she was always right. If he showed up to the council with her, there'd be hell to pay.

Well, what am I supposed to tell the humans?

Do they suspect us?

No. When I left Aspen, her parents had arrived, and they were talking about searching for a bear or wolf pack.

Then tell them nothing. No reason to let them think that one of us can't control his appetite. It would cause too much drama.

I am the king. Don't I get some say in this?

King or no, you don't have the right to rule until you finish this wretched experience and take your queen. Right now, the council decides what will be done about this renegade dragon.

Sid clenched his fists. She was right again. But that didn't change the fact that more could die if the dragons didn't tell them. They could at least warn them to close down the parks until the dragons took care of their own problem.

I still think the humans should know. Wouldn't it be better to tell them than to let them witness it firsthand? I don't think this is the first human that has been eaten by him. He's not going to stop.

That's not your decision to make. Give me two days, and I'll come back and let you know what we decide. Can you wait until then?

No, Sid said, sulking.

Pearl spread her wings, spanning the width of the driveway, preparing to take flight.

I am only looking out for you. You need to make it out of this alive. Take care of yourself. This isn't the first emergency we've ever dealt with. Don't worry. Everything will be okay.

She took off and air rushed around him, smelling of the pine trees from the yard. Sid watched her retreating back and continued worrying. He worried for his human companions who were in danger, he worried for the dragon that was doing this because he knew his fate, but most of all, he worried about his ability to be a good king. He didn't know how to handle any of this.

The house behind him was silent. Theo hadn't come outside. Sid sat on the edge of the pond and whistled, summoning the eagles. After a few moments, Talbot came into view, his wings opened wide and his bright yellow beak sticking out in contrast to his white head. Sid sighed, relieved it was him and not one of his brothers. For this task, he trusted only him. Talbot was Sid's eagle, assigned to him the moment he became king.

You called, Your Majesty. Talbot landed on the ground in front of Sid, bowing his head. Sid stroked the feathers on his neck, and Talbot looked up.

"There is a dragon attacking the humans. I need you to keep your eyes open and report anything you see to me. Have the other birds help you. I want to know who is doing this."

Of course, Your Majesty. I will report anything the birds have seen. Will there be anything else?

No. Let me know what you see.

Talbot leapt and flew into the night sky. Sid watched until he became as small as the stars, breathing a little easier, glad he could at least do this.

CHAPTER 14

TORI SHOWED UP at seven on the dot. Aspen had forgotten she was coming over. Clearly, she hadn't heard the news. No one was in the mood for games.

"You okay?" Tori asked, pushing past her into the house.

Aspen shook her head. "Something happened today." Aspen didn't know what to tell her. Matt's parents had been notified, but Aspen didn't know who else knew.

Aspen followed Tori into the living room. Her parents both looked up.

"I forgot I invited Tori to game night."

Aspen's mom, Stacey, smiled a tight smile. "It's okay. Come sit."

Tori threw herself on a bean bag chair. "What happened? Everyone looks like death."

Aspen's dad, Jason, started to talk, but Aspen knew she had to be the one to tell Tori.

"Matt died today. I found him." Aspen almost said, "Sid and I found him," but she knew Tori would take that the wrong way. Even in the midst of death, Tori would find some way to make it about her.

Tori's eyes widened. "What? How?"

"I was out hiking, and when I came back to the main road, I found his body. Well, sort of."

Tori dropped her eyes. "What do you mean sort of?"

Jason spoke up. "His arm was the only part of his body they found."

Tori's eyes narrowed. "Dragons?"

Rowan nodded. "That's what I said too. But Aspen won't hear of it."

Aspen threw her arms up. "That would be your first reaction."

"Because that's the only explanation." Tori stood and started pacing. "Is there evidence the body was dragged away?"

Jason shook his head. "No. But that doesn't mean anything. It could be a wolf pack or bears. For all we know, it's a human. Whatever it is, it's dangerous. That's the second body in two weeks. Aspen, I want your keys."

"What? No."

"Yes. I've already talked to your principal. School's been cancelled for the rest of the week. You're the only one rash enough to go hiking. The park is closing for tourists for a few weeks, but you know how to get around. Keys."

"Tori's not the only one who's going to suspect the dragons. I need to prove they're innocent. I can't do that by staying cooped up in my room."

Stacey laughed. "And exactly how are you going to do that?"

"By getting close to them. If I can prove they are friendly with humans, then maybe jumping to this conclusion every time someone dies in a national park will stop. This isn't the first time."

Jason frowned. "Girls. Sit down, please. You're making me nervous." Aspen and Tori glared at each other and sat. "I know people unfairly accuse the dragons of a lot of things, but this is one of those situations where I think Tori might be right. These are the most unusual park disappearances I've ever seen. I'm usually the first one called when there is a death, so I've seen a lot. The areas around the body parts were clean, and we couldn't find any animals tracks. Truthfully, I think this is either the work of a dragon or a serial killer. You tell me which sounds more probable."

"Serial killer," Aspen said at the same time Tori said, "Dragons."

Jason shook his head. "Either way, it's dangerous. You're staying home."

Aspen dug her keys out of her purse and tossed them to him. This would blow over. Besides, she was more resourceful than that. She could find a way out. Her bigger problem was the dragons. There had been times over the years where people decided the dragons needed to be taken out because they were dangerous, but never in Aspen's lifetime. As far as she knew, nothing ever came of those instances. She didn't want to witness the first dragon killing in centuries. She had to prove they were friendly. That meant she had to get close enough to touch one again.

Everyone sat in silence for a few seconds. No one was talking about the real problem. Matt was dead. A knot formed in Aspen's chest. She hadn't been interested in him, but he was still her friend. Finally, Stacey spoke up.

"Do you all want to play Skipbo? It will take our mind off things."

Everyone murmured their assent, and within fifteen minutes, things were almost back to normal. There was still an air of sadness, but Aspen and Tori spoke to each other like the fight they had never happened. Dragons weren't mentioned again.

CHAPTER 15

GETTING OUT OF the house proved difficult. The next afternoon, Aspen knocked on Rowan's bedroom door.

"Come in," he yelled. Aspen cracked his door open and peeked inside. With the exception of the gaming chair, his room looked like a stark hotel room. No pictures hung on the walls, the desk spotless, and his bed was so tightly made up that a military general would approve. His messy blonde head bobbed in tune with his music, and he stared intently at the video game on his TV.

After a few minutes, the screen flashed game over, and he turned to look at Aspen. Square spectacles covered his eyes that were green like hers, but bigger. Why did boys always get the pretty eye gene? It wasn't fair.

"What's up?"

"I'm going stir crazy. Wanna go for a drive?"

"No." He got up and thumbed through a book of DVDs.

"Come on. Please."

"The last time we went for a drive, I ended up standing at the bottom of a mountain for three hours praying you wouldn't fall off. They had to up my anxiety meds by 200 milligrams for the next month. I'm not interested in experiencing that again."

"You never told me that."

He shrugged. "I didn't want you to feel guilty."

Rowan had been slightly off kilter since they were young. Aspen wasn't the only twin to meander off in the Everglades as a toddler. They were both adventurous. Something happened one day when he wandered off by himself. They were six. When Rowan came back, he was paranoid. He never talked about it to anyone. Not even Aspen.

The rest of the time they lived in the Everglades, he only went outside if an adult was with him, and if Aspen ever went exploring on her own, he would rock back and forth in terror in his room until she got home.

For a while her parents tried to get help for him, but nothing worked. Eventually they accepted Rowan's odd behavior and medicated him. Aspen was the only one who still remembered what Rowan was like before he became a pussy cat.

In spite of that, they were still got along pretty well. They watched geek movies and played video games together but never talked about his issues. Aspen did her best to respect them, but sometimes she pushed him a little because she wanted him to be normal. She had no idea the day she went rappelling she had hurt him.

The clock was ticking. If Aspen wanted to get out of the house before dark, she had to act fast. That dragon would be there at sunset, and every second she begged, she risked losing the opportunity to see it.

"We won't even get out of the car. We'll just drive." Lies, lies, lies.

"Not a good idea today. I didn't take my meds this morning."

"Why?" Aspen asked, dumfounded. "You've been on meds for ten years. Why would you forget today?" She sank down on his bed, knowing the dragon would appear without her. Getting Rowan out of the house in this state of mind would be impossible. Her parent's made it clear that if she wanted her keys, Rowan would have to go with her.

"I didn't forget. I chose not to."

"Why?"

"Matt died."

Aspen's stomach clenched. She'd been trying not to think about it. Dragons were a good diversion.

"What does that have to do with anything?"

Rowan turned his chair to face her, and she sat. "Do you know what those meds do to me?"

"No," Aspen said honestly.

"They remove my ability to feel. Anything. When Mom told me about Matt, I should've felt sad or scared or something, but I didn't. I'm an empty shell. I don't want to live like that forever. Life was meant to be experienced, not feared. If death came for me tomorrow, I'd have lived an artificial life. I'm not ready to die like that."

Whoa. "Did you tell Mom and Dad you stopped taking your meds?"

He shook his head. "Will you help me?"

"Of course, but you know living actually means you have to leave the house." The sun was already setting; it made no sense to try to find the dragon tonight. "Will you go for a drive with me tomorrow?"

He nodded, but a sheen of sweat appeared on his forehead.

The next night Aspen's parents let them go. Getting Rowan out of the house was more difficult than Aspen anticipated. By the time they drove away from their house, the sun was low in the sky. Rowan shook in the passenger seat, not saying a word. She tried not to think about what it would do to him when she left him in the car in search of the dragon. But Rowan was her only chance for getting out of the house. A few miles from the trail Sid showed her, the car sputtered.

"What the," she muttered.

"What's going on?" Rowan squeaked.

"Nothing." Aspen pushed the accelerator, but the car slowed down.

She pulled the car into the grass and pounded the steering wheel, cursing. Would she ever manage to see the dragon that probably wasn't there because Sid couldn't possibly know what he was talking about? But still, she had to know. The sun had dropped below the horizon, and within a half hour, it would be completely dark. Even if she ran, she wouldn't make it.

"Stupid effing car," Aspen yelled and put her head on the steering wheel. She couldn't believe she ran out of gas.

Rowan moaned next to her. He had brought his legs up into a fetal position and rocked back and forth. He looked at her, his eyes wide with fright.

"You okay?" Aspen asked, knowing how stupid that sounded. Of course he wasn't okay.

He didn't respond.

"Look, nothing's going to happen. I'll call Mom and Dad, and they'll come get us. No biggie."

Mom and Dad weren't quite so understanding. They still didn't know Rowan stopped taking the meds, and they questioned Aspen for hours after they towed her car home as to what she did that scared him so badly.

For some reason, "letting my car run out of gas," didn't seem like a big enough reason for them.

CHAPTER 16

ON FRIDAY THEY finally had school again. It was supposed to be on Monday, but the funeral had been on Thursday, and the school board agreed that getting back to normal was the best thing for the kids.

Aspen hadn't taken the bait. For the past three nights Sid flew out to the pond and waited. Technically, Sid wasn't supposed to be in dragon form. But he didn't know how else to win over Aspen. He was careful and only flew in areas where he knew most dragons didn't frequent. Besides, the dragons were busy looking for the human killer.

But Aspen never showed.

A lot of students were absent that day, and so Sid was surprised to see Aspen slip into math a few minutes late. She didn't seem to like school, and he thought she'd take any excuse to stay home. Although, if she was anything like him, she'd been going stir crazy the last couple of days.

During class, she held her head so still and did not look back, even if a friend or Mrs. Weber called her name from behind. Once again

Sid envied the canyon dragons. Being one of them, he could have simply heard her thoughts, but no, he had been blessed with feelings. She tried so hard not to look at him, her long neck tense. Her hands shook when she opened her notebook. Sid couldn't help himself. He leaned forward and whispered in her ear, "Hey Aspen."

She shivered and spun around, eyes blazing and nostrils flaring.

"Could you not talk to me? Please. Can you just leave me alone for one day?" She gathered her things, shoved them into her bag, and stormed out the room.

At lunch, Sid sat with Tori, Dan, and Lila. Wispy clouds drifted across the otherwise bright sky, and the outdoor lunchroom was crowded. Soon, it would be too cold to use it, so everyone took advantage of the nice weather.

Tori kept scooting closer to him, and he kept moving away. Soon, he would be on the ground. Aspen came outside a few minutes after him and sat on the other side of Dan, which was about as far away as she could get from him and still sit with her friends.

Sid was trying to listen to the conversation between Aspen and Dan, but Tori kept distracting him.

"There was a press conference held this morning about the killings in the park," said Dan.

"I know. They're starting to talk about the dragons. I've got to fix this."

Dan snorted. "How are you going to fix it?"

"Prove that dragons aren't dangerous."

Tori stopped trying to climb into Sid's lap. "Yes, they are. They should be killed. Every single one of them. Everyone knows that but you."

Aspen's anger flared. "How could you say that? Humans kill each other every day, and no one is calling for a mass extermination of us. Yet, two people die in the national park and people assume it's the dragons with absolutely no proof, and suddenly everyone wants to kill them."

Aspen grabbed her bag and stormed over to the other side of the courtyard. The potential for war with the humans bothered Sid, but he knew their ambassadors would smooth things over. He wished he could tell Aspen everything would be okay, but then he'd have a lot more explaining to do.

Pearl's voice suddenly filled his head, startling him. *I need to talk to you.*

Where are you? he asked.

Down the street. I'll be there in a minute.

Are you driving or flying?

Flying.

Sid nearly laughed out loud. He got up and moved away from the table. *You know I'm sitting in a courtyard with several humans, right? How do you think they're going to react when they see you? Especially now.*

Doesn't matter. I've spoken to the council about the boy who was eaten. I promised I would let you know what was decided.

Why are you coming so close? You could tell me from there.

Because I want to see you. I'll be going away for a while, and I'm going to miss you.

This would be interesting. Pearl being out in public and so close to people was going to cause an uproar. Sid stood and watched the sky.

"Hey, Sid, whatcha looking at?" Tori jumped up next to him. She leaned into him, and he moved.

"Nothing," he replied. Tori looked up and saw Pearl at the same time he did. Pearl's silver wings reflected the sunlight like mirrors, sending light fragments all over the courtyard. She was a tall dragon with a long neck and slender body.

Tori screamed. Sid's ears rung. By the time her scream died down, everyone had seen the dragon. Lunches were left on tables, and people scrambled inside. Sid's own body froze with the fear surrounding him. Tori pushed him out of the way and ran for the door. By the time Pearl came to rest on the roof, everyone had gone inside but Aspen, who had eyes only for Pearl.

Aspen had her camera out and was furiously taking pictures. Excitement rolled off her, and Sid's heart raced.

Pearl, could you give her a show? Sid asked.

Pearl rolled her gigantic eyes. *If it were anyone but you asking, little brother, I'd take his head off. I'm guessing that's Aspen. She's got guts.*

Pearl took off again and loop-de-looped in the air. Sid kept his eyes on Aspen as Pearl continued to chatter in his head.

We aren't going to let the humans know what's going on. We'll find this dragon and deal with him on our own. We'll patrol the area and find him before he...

Sid stopped listening to her. Aspen's knot on the back of her head came loose. It hung in between her shoulder blades, resting on her red tank top, and Sid noticed for the first time that she wore short denim shorts revealing long bronze legs. He couldn't see her face. The camera obscured it.

His heart fluttered, and his stomach flooded with warmth. She was stunning, and he longed to have her. His head buzzed as he moved toward her. More than anything he wanted to stand at her side, to be in her space, to hold her. Sid wanted to see Pearl as Aspen did. Her passion became his, and he never wanted to be away from her.

Without stopping to think about what he was doing, Sid sealed himself to Aspen.

Unfortunately, Pearl felt it too.

Sid, she screamed.

I know, Sid said. *I know. I didn't mean for this to happen.* His ankle burned and tingled.

Pearl landed in front of him, sending tables end over end. She tossed her head and roared.

Are you insane? What did you think would happen? You've been mooning after her for the last week and a half. Did you think you'd be able to walk away from her once she started talking to you? You idiot. You are going to ruin this for everyone. What if you blow this and Marcellus becomes king? Huh? Then what?

She flung her tail from side to side and stomped her feet, crushing the ground beneath her. Hamburgers and Cokes went flying. Aspen, somehow unaware of Pearl's anger, still snapped away. Aspen moved forward and touched Pearl's wing.

She snarled, and Aspen backed away. Aspen stumbled and lifted her foot briefly, a puzzled look on her face.

Look at her. She thinks I'm her pet. Do I look like a pet to you? How could you do this? You had over a hundred and fifty years with Skye and you never let your guard down, yet in less than three weeks you pledge your undying love to this one?

I didn't plan this. Sid started to sweat, and he couldn't think straight, unable to tell whether the panic he felt was his own or Pearl's.

That much is obvious. Have you planned anything recently? It's time you got your priorities straight. You are no longer free to live out your little fantasies. You are here for one purpose and one purpose only, to prepare for your reign. Focus and lose the girl or I'll find a way to lose her for you. I'm going to see if we can transfer you someplace else. Don't do anything reckless while I'm gone. And stay away from that girl. As long as her feelings don't change, you can still be king.

I can take care of this myself, Sid said.

You'd better. You really are shaping up to be a lousy king. I had hoped for better things from you. She let loose a volley of flames and took off.

Sid watched her retreat and fought the urge to yell childish retorts.

"Amazing," Aspen said behind him. For a brief moment he'd forgotten about her.

Her hair fell in blonde waves to her hips. As he walked toward her, he reveled in the tingling in his limbs, the butterflies in his stomach, the buzzing in his head. Love. It was intoxicating. Why would he run from that? He'd never felt so alive in his life. Who cared what Pearl said? He wasn't about to lose this. Aspen wasn't aware of his presence. Sid walked up behind her, and she turned to face him. Her face flushed, smiling. She smelled the same as she did on the mountain, of adrenaline and roses.

"Did you see her?" she asked.

"Yeah."

"I can't believe she perched right on the school, did all those acrobatics and then the flames. Here look." She showed him the picture on her camera. "It was almost like she wanted me to take her picture."

"Yeah," Sid said. He couldn't think of anything else to say. He was shocked she was talking to him, and he was afraid if he alerted her that he was Sid, she would stop.

She continued flipping through the pictures. A door opened behind them, and Aspen looked up. But Sid didn't take his eyes off her.

"Oh, Mrs. Dufour, look," Aspen rushed over to the teacher and showed her the pictures.

"Pictures! I don't want to look at pictures," Mrs. Dufour said. "You could have been killed, you too, Mr. King. What were you thinking?"

"Don't you see? This proves they aren't dangerous. She came so close to us and didn't hurt anyone."

"Then you somehow didn't see the same thing I did. She nearly bit your head off. They've never come into town before. They've had a taste of human flesh, and now they are searching for it."

Aspen sputtered.

"Dragons are not dangerous," Sid said and walked inside. The spell Aspen cast over him had broken when Mrs. Dufour came out, and he realized how much trouble he was getting himself into. He needed time to think away from the long hair and blazing eyes, to absorb what had happened to him.

Theo waited with his arms crossed on a bench next to the fountain. The shadow from the house fell upon him. Sid felt disappointment when he climbed out of the car. He put his backpack down, hesitating. In human years, Theo was twenty-eight, but today he looked much older with lines etched around his eyes and forehead. Sid sat next to him and dipped his fingers in the water.

"What are you going to do?" Theo asked.

"About Aspen?"

Theo snorted. "Who else?"

"I'm not sure there's anything I can do."

"That's stupid. Of course there's stuff you can do. Like let's see, how about starting with 'stay away from Aspen,' and then you could always 'stay away from Aspen.' Of course you could always try 'staying away from Aspen.' Still think there's nothing you can do?"

It's not that easy.

Yes, it is.

You weren't supposed to hear that.

Why are you letting your mental guard down? When's the last time that happened? When you were ten? You're falling apart.

Theo was right. Sid needed to pull himself together. Especially considering he had to work with Aspen tonight.

"You're not going to work. I've already talked to Ella." Theo picked up a stone from the driveway and chucked it out into the lawn.

"Stop listening to my thoughts."

"You're broadcasting them. Get a grip."

"Why am I not going to work tonight?"

"I thought I made myself clear. Because you need to stay away from Aspen."

Shouts of protest followed Sid to his car and became muffled when he slammed the door shut. But Sid didn't go to work. If Theo already called in, he would use the time to think. He drove into Yellowstone, spotted a little used trailhead, and pulled off the road.

He climbed. The path was steep and narrow. Trees stretched out for miles on either side of him. He could feel the animals follow- ing him. The bears, the birds, the wolves, and the foxes. Sid didn't see them. They kept their distance. They recognized him as their king even if the dragons thought he needed to wait a few years. He built a shield in his mind like Skye taught him years ago. He didn't allow any thoughts out or in.

Sid lay on the grass, the cool ground soothing his sorrows. He closed his eyes and released his shield. His mind expanded, and he pushed out the mental borders so he could hear the broadcasts of the other animals. A mother bear instructed her cubs on the best way to catch a fish, an owl argued with an eagle over a mouse. Sid pushed his mind farther and discovered the ants were nearly ready for winter and that the fish knew how to avoid sharp claws. They all whispered of him.

One by one he shut the conversations off. Click, no ants. Click, no owl. Click, no more mother bear. Soon he was left alone to think. He practiced this exercise many times over the years. Unbeknownst to Theo, he'd never been particularly good at keeping his thoughts to himself. It was something animals had to learn and the first thing his mother taught him, but he never fully perfected it until he met Skye. Humans were one of only a few species on the planet who actually had to make a conscious effort to send out thought.

Sid opened his eyes and found a wolf cub nose to nose with him. The cub blinked and ran away. Sid sat up and saw he was surrounded. The animals had come to see their new and mighty dragon king.

They ran away when he sat up, most likely not wanting to disturb him. He was utterly alone in the woods, and his mind shut off once again. Sid finally understood how it was that humans could feel so complex. He loved Aspen, more than anything. But he could not allow himself to indulge that feeling or to pursue it. If she ever felt the same way, he'd be dead the minute the council discovered it. So while he felt like he was in paradise, he was also in hell.

Sid wanted to see the etching that sealed him to her. As long as it remained a swirl of loops and patterns, he was technically still okay. If her name were to show up, it would be over. At the moment, that wouldn't be a problem.

He peeled away his sock and looked at his etching for the first time. The loops and swirls were there, but in the midst of them a single word was scrawled.

Aspen.

CHAPTER 17

NOT ONE WORD, but six. Her name was on the front and back of his ankle and in between was the scrawling of the ancient dragon language.

Aspen ~ Nin Bereth ~ Aspen ~ Nin Meleth

He'd have to look the meanings up when he got home.

Death was coming. The only question was how soon. He probably had until Pearl came back, as long as no one else realized Aspen had sealed herself to him. That could take days, months, or even years.

Pearl had to find a way to call a full council and convince them to transfer him without revealing why. She was resourceful but would need help, and Sid hoped she wasn't desperate enough to involve someone else.

Sid paced among the trees and considered his options, limited as they were. They all ended the same, with the dragon council tearing apart his body. Sitting around and waiting for them to come seemed wasteful somehow. So he chose the only option that made sense.

When he got home, the house was quiet. Usually, Theo watched television in the living room, but tonight silence reigned.

Sid crept up the stairs, unsure why he was being sneaky. Noises came from Theo's room, and he approached the door and listened. A female voice giggled. "I'll be right back."

Ella bounded out of Theo's room and into Sid's arms. "Oops, sorry. What're you doing out here?"

"Nothing, I just got home."

"Which way to the bathroom?"

Sid pointed down the hall. Ella, wrapped in a sheet, shuffled toward the bathroom. Anger rose in him like never before. He stormed into Theo's room.

"Dude, what the…" Theo hurried to cover himself up. The room was a mess. Pillows, blankets, and sheets were everywhere.

"What the hell are you doing?"

"Nothing, I, oh man, Sid, you don't understand."

"I understand perfectly well. Number one rule, no sex with humans. We mate for life. You just ruined your chances for parenthood."

"Rule number two, actually, not sealing yourself to a human is number one. And I only ruined my chances if the council finds out."

"Technicality." Sid closed his eyes and took several deep breaths. The nerve Theo had, mating with a human. Sid tried to think of a way to fix this, to make it disappear. Several decades ago a cousin had mated with a human. He nearly married her, until his mentor found out and reported him to the council. Sid watched, along with Theo and the other potential kings, while the king tore him to pieces. His head landed right in front of Sid.

Sid's death sentence was already written since eventually his sins would be known because the sealing couldn't be hidden for long. Theo had a life to live. His sin was a secret. No one had to know. Plus, Theo needed to be here with him. He couldn't risk anyone else finding out about Aspen.

"Are you saying you don't love her?"

"Of course not, I barely know her. She knows that. She doesn't love me either."

"Then why are you mating with her?"

"Sid, I know you don't get it. But sex is different for humans. They don't mate for life, and it's not about kids. It's about desire, excitement, and fun."

"But what about the rules? And what if someone finds out? You'll be killed."

"I spent the last ten years denying this desire so I could be ready to be king. Then you become king, and I'm told I have to come back to this wretched human form for another ten years to watch over you. Sorry, I'm done following the rules. No one's going to find out unless you tell them."

"What if I do?"

Theo glared at Sid. "You wouldn't."

As angry as Sid wanted to be with Theo, he was pleased with how well this fit into his plans. Although Aspen had obviously sealed herself to him, she didn't seem all that keen to be around him.

"I'm going to pursue this thing with Aspen, and you are going to keep me out of trouble. You will help me win her over, and you'll keep your mouth shut about love."

"Obsidian, you're the king. You can't do that."

"Then you can't have sex."

Ella toddled into the room. "Sorry, I didn't mean to interrupt. I'll just get my clothes and leave."

Theo's eyes burned as he watched her scurry around the room. "Ella, stay. Sid is leaving."

She leaned over to pick up a pillow, and her sheet slipped, revealing a fairy tattoo.

Theo turned to Sid. "I won't say anything, but I'm not helping you."

Ella threw the pillow onto the bed and sat, hiking the sheet up to cover her chest. "What won't you tell? I want to know."

"Sid's in love with Aspen."

Ella grinned. "Yeah, I know. It's time he figured it out. You are going to help and so am I. Starting tonight."

CHAPTER 18

S ID DESERVED TO die a thousand deaths. The hike to the top of the hill took forty-five minutes, and Aspen had misjudged the steepness so she didn't have any of her gear. The result was bloody palms and a head full of briars. Which would've been worth it if the dragon had actually shown up. But, of course, he didn't, because Sid was an idiot who didn't know what he was talking about.

Aspen made it back to her car about nine o'clock, tired and grumpy. Her phone buzzed just before she started the car. Ella.

What u doin tn?

IDK yet. Figuring stuff out.

A surprise 4 u. u want it? Ella's surprise could be just about anything.

Sure.

Ok, I'll be over in 30 or less. Dress sexy.

Yes! Ella was finally going to take her clubbing. Aspen had been begging her for months; Ella knew all the best places, but she needed to get Aspen an ID first. Dancing would be perfect to burn off the anger.

After Aspen sped home, she showered and contemplated her wardrobe. The only time she ended up with sexy was when she went shopping with Tori, and all those clothes still had the tags.

Aspen found a black long sleeved mini dress with a print of a silver dragon. She loved it the moment she saw it. The back of the dress had the body and the wings of the dragon with the head and tail entangled on the front. Aspen never even tried the dress on, just bought it straight off the rack knowing that no way in hades would she ever wear it. Tonight seemed appropriate.

The dress was short and revealed far more cleavage than she'd shown in ages. But, she reasoned, everyone else would be wearing clothes equally revealing. Probably more. Aspen left her hair down and dug among her shoes for the boots Tori bought for her birthday. They wouldn't go with her thick socks on. She'd never taken her socks off since that dragon marked her, except in the shower. She shrugged. She'd just need to remember to put another pair of socks on before she went to bed, in case her parents came in while she was sleeping and her foot was sticking out.

She'd never worn the boots before. The three-inch heels went clear above the knee. A touch of eye shadow and mascara and the effect was complete. Sexy. Ella would be pleased.

Ella whistled as Aspen got into the car. "I didn't think you'd listen to me."

"I can listen sometimes. Can I see my ID?"

"What ID?"

"You're taking me clubbing right?"

Ella laughed and sped toward town. "Sorry, chica, I've got other plans for us."

Aspen probed, but couldn't get another word out of her. They drove through town, past the coffee shop, and turned down Shelby Lane.

Aspen's fingers curled around the edge of her seat as Ella parked in front the gigantic home. Aspen hit the lock button when Ella left the car and looked away, but she had a keyless remote, so in less than thirty seconds she had the door opened and Aspen's seatbelt off.

Aspen glared at her. "I'm not getting out."

"Come on, it's not that bad."

"Yes, it is. You said nothing about your 'surprise' involving Sid."

Aspen was a little bit curious. No one she knew had set foot in King's Castle before. They'd all heard about it, and she'd snuck over the gates a couple of times, but had never actually been inside the house, er, castle.

The weathered stone mansion looked like it should be perched on a cliff in Ireland. Towers stood tall on both sides of the main house. They had to be four, five stories tall. Aspen wanted to see the inside, but she wasn't getting out of the car.

"Why are we here?"

"Theo and Sid wanted to make dinner for me, and I didn't want Sid to feel like the odd man out."

"So you invited me?"

"Yeah."

"Ella, I don't like Sid."

Ella rolled her eyes. "This isn't a date. We're just having dinner."

"You told me to dress sexy."

"That was for Sid's benefit, not yours. You do look good. I should tell you to dress sexy more often." Ella laughed.

"It's not funny. Take me home."

Ella crouched next to the car, not an easy feat since her outfit was shorter than Aspen's.

"I really like Theo. He feels like he's leaving Sid out. This was the only way I could see him tonight. Do this for me, please."

She turned on her Bambi eyes. The ones Aspen could never resist, which was how she ended up working a ton of overtime at the Purple Dragon.

"Fine," Aspen mumbled and got out of the car, angry at that small part of herself that actually wanted to be here. "But you owe me."

Ella let herself in the front door without knocking. At the end of the enormous entrance hall, two sets of stairs wound up to a landing. The marble floors gleamed.

"Pretty cool, huh," Ella said.

"Yeah."

She led Aspen past the right set of stairs and into the kitchen. A marble island in the middle of the room sparkled. Double ovens were built into the walls, and next to those was the sink. Not a single appliance was turned on.

Both Sid and Theo were sitting on the island, grinning. They had been talking until the girls entered the room. Ella wasted no time once she saw Theo. She was in his arms, and their lips locked together in less than ten seconds.

"I thought Ella said you two were making dinner," Aspen said loudly, trying to squash the steam that Ella and Theo seemed intent on.

Theo grimaced. "We were, but after Ella left, we realized that neither one of us knew how to cook, so we ordered delivery. The pizza guy should be here soon."

The doorbell rang.

"Sid, why don't you go get the pizza, and I'll show the girls into the theater room."

Sid slid off the counter and left the room without saying anything to Aspen. He kept his head down and wouldn't look at her. Aspen knew she hadn't been nice to him, but still.

Theo had his arm around Ella, and he reached for Aspen's hand. He spun her in a circle and whistled. "Sid's got good taste, dragon girl. You look hot."

Aspen blushed, unsure of how to take the compliment. Ella grinned, so Aspen supposed it was okay. He put his other arm around Aspen. "This way, ladies."

Aspen counted doors; there were six ways out of the kitchen. Theo shuttled them down a long hallway, under an archway, and up a short set of stairs.

"Relax. Take off your shoes," Theo said.

Aspen paused. She didn't have socks on, but her parents weren't here to see the tattoo. Besides, what was she going to do? Wear those stupid boots all through the movie. The lighting was low enough that maybe no one would notice. Ella wouldn't tell her parents anyway. Aspen slipped off her boots. For some reason, she felt less exposed without them on. They stepped into the room and onto sinking velvet carpet. Ella laughed. "How come I haven't seen this room yet?"

"'Cause I like my bedroom better." Theo kissed her, for a long time. In the extreme awkwardness, Aspen wished Sid would come back. She didn't like being around people who were overly affectionate, and so she wandered farther into the room.

An oversized couch formed a U around an eight-foot ottoman covered in bowls filled with chips, pretzels, M&Ms, and popcorn. On the floor was a cooler of ice with all kinds of sodas. Sid appeared in front of Aspen, carrying five pizza boxes. "You like junk food, right?"

"Of course." Aspen crossed her arms over her chest.

"Where are Theo and Ella?"

"They got tied up by the door."

Sid glanced their direction, and a dark look passed over his face. Then he turned to Aspen. "You wanna pick the movie?"

"Movie?" Aspen didn't see a TV anywhere. Sid motioned for her to follow and opened a door. He flipped a switch and walked in. The room looked like a library, but instead of books, it had thousands of movies.

"What do you like?"

"Action, adventure, blowing things up."

"Really?"

"I hope you don't think I'm a sucker for cheesy romantic movies like *Titanic* or *Pretty Woman*." So what if she could quote *The Notebook* by heart, no one else had to know.

"No, I just didn't quite picture you as the blowing-things-up type, but maybe it will prevent Theo and Ella from pawing each other all night." Sid pointed to the shelf next to her, and she scanned the titles. Aspen debated between *Die Hard* and *The Matrix* and finally handed Sid both. "I can't decide."

"I haven't seen either one."

"Then you've been deprived." Aspen took both movies from him, put *Die Hard* on the shelf, and plucked out the other two *Matrix* movies.

"Looks like it's going to be a long night for you. You'll need to watch all three. In case I zonk out before the movies are over, *Reloaded* comes before *Revolution*."

Aspen walked into the room and opened one of the pizza boxes, ignoring her racing heart. She hated the way he made her feel. Being near him felt natural, yet wrong. She yelled over her shoulder, "Hey, Ella, the pizza's gonna get cold."

"I think we've been ditched." Sid came back carrying a remote.

"Uh-oh, who's going to eat all the food? We should invite a few others." Aspen didn't want to be alone with him.

He sat down next her, too close for her comfort. "Like who?"

"I'll call Tori. She can always come up with a few people."

"I'd rather you didn't."

"Why not? You know I'm not all that comfortable being alone with you."

He shrugged. "Don't take this the wrong way or anything, but I don't really like Tori. I'm sure she's a nice girl and all, but it's painfully obvious she likes me, and that makes her difficult to be around.

I've told her in no uncertain terms I'm not interested, and she won't back off."

"Sid, you are aware how hypocritical that is?"

He looked surprised. "Oh, you mean us? Well, I wouldn't be sitting in her living room alone with her, so I guess that makes us different. You like me. You're just not ready to admit it yet."

Aspen moved away from him and rose from the couch. "I'm leaving."

He grabbed her hand. "No, wait, I'm sorry. That didn't come out right. Please stay. We'll watch these movies you seem to think are so great, and I'll be good. I promise. I'll even sit on the opposite side of the couch from you. Please." He pushed a button on the remote, and the entire wall in front of the couch lit up with the DVD menu from the movie. The floor shook with the sound. Aspen had never watched a movie like that.

She sat on the edge of the couch as far away from him as possible. "I'm sitting here. You stay over there."

He nodded but got up and walked to the closet. He came back carrying a blanket. "You're shivering," he said, spreading a quilt over Aspen. It smelled old but had a pattern of red dragons on it.

"This is gorgeous. Where did you get it?"

"My mother made it."

Where were his parents anyway? It seemed strange that he was living here with just his brother. Aspen almost asked but then decided it wouldn't be worth the conversation.

They gorged on pizza and pretzels through the first movie. Aspen had to explain most of it to him, and he slowly migrated to her side of the couch. She didn't even notice.

At the end Sid got up to change the DVD.

"If Ella doesn't come back down, will you give me a ride home?"

"Sure, can I ask you a strange question?"

"Yeah."

"Does this whole Ella and Theo thing bother you?"

"Why would it?"

"I don't know. They barely know each other, but they're already having sex. It doesn't seem right."

Of all things he could've said, that one shocked Aspen the most. What did he care if they were having sex or not?

"So? It's not unusual. It won't last of course, but I think they both know that."

"Yeah, but, I don't know. I always thought love was a prerequisite. Ya know?"

The closet romantic inside Aspen's head had a sudden desire to kiss him. She hated the way he managed to do that when she was least expecting it. In class the first time they'd met, at the Purple Dragon when he'd walked her to the car, and any other time when she forgot, for a nanosecond, that he looked like Marc. He sat down next to her. Aspen leaned closer to him, wanting to reach out and touch his lips.

"May I see your tattoo?" he asked, startling her.

"My what?"

"Your tattoo, the one on your ankle."

"Oh, sure." Until tonight, she'd been super careful about keeping the tat covered. Sid was the first person to see it, and she wanted to show it off a bit.

He slid onto the floor and pulled her foot into his lap. Shivers ran up her spine. He slowly traced the words with his finger and whispered under his breath.

"Obsidian, Nin Meleth, Nin Aran."

Aspen's first instinct was to pull her foot away, but she enjoyed it as much as it tortured her. She bit her lip and waited for him let go. Instead, he adjusted so that he could see her, but he continued to hold her foot in his lap.

"When did you get this?" he asked.

"Um, about a month ago. It's not really a tattoo."

He raised his eyebrows.

"It's gonna sound crazy, but it's a dragon marking. It appeared when I touched that black dragon, but it didn't have all those words, only a bunch of loops. Then today, when I touched that silver dragon in the courtyard, it changed. The only word that makes sense is Obsidian. I think that might be the name of the silver dragon."

He pursed his lips. "Maybe. But it would make more sense if it was the name of the black one."

Aspen hadn't thought of that. "Why?"

"Because Obsidian is a black rock, not a silver one."

"Oh." Now she felt silly.

He let go of her foot, moved onto the couch, and pressed the play button on the remote.

About halfway through the movie, her eyes refused to stay open. After fighting with them for fifteen minutes, she gave in, allowed them to close, and settled her head into a soft warm pillow.

Ella shook her awake. "Aspen," she whispered. "We need to go."

"No," Aspen said and closed her eyes.

Ella shook Aspen again. "Come on, we've got to leave. You can't stay here."

"Yes, she can," Aspen's pillow said.

"I was trying not to wake you up, Sid," Ella said. "I'm sorry."

"No worries." He brushed hair out of Aspen's face.

Aspen shot up, embarrassed. She stumbled around the couch looking for her boots. Ella handed them to her. "Here ya go."

"Thanks," Aspen mumbled.

Aspen fumed. His lap was not where her head should have been. In fact, he shouldn't have even been sitting next to her. Tori was going to be furious. If Aspen told her. Which she wouldn't.

CHAPTER 19

S ID FOLLOWED ELLA and Aspen out to the car. Aspen ignored him and slammed the car door shut, but Ella lingered for a moment. She looped her arm through Sid's and rested her head on his shoulder. She stared in through her car window at Aspen, who had her arms crossed and was facing away.

"Her subconscious likes you. She'll come around."

"I'd rather her conscious self like me."

Ella laughed. "Yeah, me too. You're scheduled to work together Sunday morning. Try to be nicer this time." She leaned up and kissed him on the cheek. "See you tomorrow."

Aspen and Ella drove away in a cloud of dust. He was tormented by the pain of watching her leave, mingled with the pleasure of finding her in his lap. If he'd had any idea the sealing was like this, he probably would've done it ages ago with Skye. But then he would've been in more trouble because he couldn't have hid it.

Sid walked out into the night air and sat on the fountain edge. The stars were bright in the clear sky since his house was dark. Theo must have gone to bed when Ella left. Aspen brushed off their relationship as nothing, and it bothered him. As dragons, they couldn't physically mate with more than one. Theo thought that as long as no one found out he'd be fine, but he wouldn't be. Theo would never be able to seal himself to anyone, except maybe Ella, but maybe not. Sid never heard of anyone mating before they were sealed. And Theo certainly killed any possibility of kids.

A dying star fell across the sky, and Sid's thoughts turned to Aspen. He had no idea she sealed herself to him the first time she saw him. He had mistaken her feelings of love for excitement. Strange things like that happened occasionally. There had been an instance with a canyon dragon whose parents had died, and he was raised by an un-sealed dragon who cared for him so much that she accidentally sealed herself to him. It wasn't a romantic love, but it was love just the same. She came to the king pleading for a solution.

He sent the dragonling to a different family and told her the seal-ing would fade over time as long she stayed away from the child. The king praised her for having the foresight to come to him before it was too late. For if the dragonling had been a few years older, he could've quite easily sealed himself back to her. Children often love their par-ents fiercely, but since their parents were already sealed to each other, the dragonlings couldn't actually become sealed to them. If the can-yon dragon had waited, she would've doomed the child to a loveless life, for she was old, only a couple hundred years away from death.

Sid figured Aspen loved Obsidian the dragon. But she despised Sid the man. The key to her heart would be as a dragon, but how did he show her they were the same? What if she hated Sid more than she loved Obsidian?

Sid shook his head, trying to sort it all out.

In the trees across the yard, he spotted Talbot and whistled.

Talbot landed in front of Sid and bowed.

Hello, Your Majesty.

Talbot, how are you? Sid stroked the feathers behind his head.

I've been better, but I'm a little embarrassed that I have failed the first mission you gave me.

No word on the dragon that's attacking humans?

No. I think the hawks know something, but they won't confide in any of us. They are very evasive. And none of us has seen any other dragons than the normal ones.

You haven't failed. You simply haven't succeeded yet. You will. I have faith in you. Can you do me one more favor?

Anything, Your Majesty.

Can you have someone keep an eye on the girl that was here with me tonight?

The wheat-colored one or the violet one?

Sid smiled at his descriptions.

Wheat. She's a good friend, and I don't want her eaten by any dragons.

He bowed and took off again, more than likely to find an eagle to watch Aspen.

CHAPTER 20

THE NEXT EVENING, at dusk, Aspen made her way down the trail she and Sid followed the day Matt died, climbed out of the trees, and began the long stretch from the field to the hill. The yellowing field dotted with buffalo and deer spread out before her. The animals moved as she walked, not allowing her to get close. She tripped over a rock and realized she should probably watch where she was going.

At her feet a sagebrush lizard skittered away. She almost followed him and reached for her camera, but then remembered she had bigger lizards to find tonight. Dusk fell rapidly, and the temperature plummeted, the cold air penetrating her light jacket.

Something flew over the mountains. A black dot, bigger than a bird, but smaller than an airplane. She paused and took out her binoculars, focusing on the flying speck. His wings were just visible. It had to be the black dragon. He landed on top of the hill and drank deeply from a pool. Aspen's heart soared. She put away her binoculars and prepared to run. He would not get away this time.

The gravel slid under her feet as she struggled to make it to the peak of the hill. She slashed at the saplings in her way and made more noise than a rampaging elephant. As she came over the top, she caught her first glimpse of him about twenty feet away.

His long neck held his head high, and his wings shimmered in the dying sunlight. Aspen's heart stuttered at the sight of him. No way was she getting away without pictures.

She approached carefully, not wanting to frighten him. He seemed bigger than she remembered. Her nose only reached the top of his knee. She looked up at his head, searching for signs he was about to take flight, but his chest rose and fell, the rest of him still.

She placed her hand on the backside of his calf.

He shivered.

Aspen flinched, expecting him to fly away, and wondered briefly what she would do if he did. Hang on to his leg probably. She waited another few moments and then reached her arms up, touched his rough kneecap, and slid both hands down his leg, feeling the scaly bumps all the way down to his foot. She traced a finger down each one of his two-foot-long ebony claws.

Then she moved her hands from his claws to his golden underbelly. He trembled as she caressed the smooth skin. Aspen grinned, ecstatic he was still there. Surrounding his left ankle was a marking like hers, but it was brilliant green instead of black. And his words were different. He had *her* name on his ankle. Her heart raced. He'd done something to connect them together. She wondered what it meant.

The dragon shifted his feet and opened his wings. Aspen stumbled backwards and moved in front of him to stare up at his face. He lowered his head, and Aspen tentatively patted his snout. Very slowly she rested her head on the top of his nose. He snorted, releasing little puffs of black smoke. Aspen backed away, coughing.

She reached around and grabbed her camera out of her pack, trying to see what would be the best angle to shoot from. She focused and saw his mouth coming toward the camera. Awesome. She shot three pictures. Then the dragon bared his teeth, and plucked her camera from her hands. He dropped the camera then stepped on it, the plastic sticking to the bottom of his foot.

"Stupid dragon, that was a $700 camera." Her stomach burned with fury. It took Aspen six months of saving her whole paycheck to buy that. Plus, any pictures of him would be gone. She had the childish impulse to run up and kick him, but she settled for crossing her arms and pouting instead.

I'm sorry. I panicked, a voice in her head said. That wasn't Aspen's voice.

She looked up at the dragon. No freaking way. "Did you just say that?" Aspen asked.

Yes. The voice was familiar somehow, but that didn't make sense because aside from the flowing thoughts, Aspen couldn't hear anything.

"You mean you can talk?" Aspen asked, flabbergasted.

In a sense, obviously, I have no vocal chords, but I can communicate with you. His voice was so real, so humanlike. Aspen wanted to dance in excitement, but she lost all feeling in her legs and sat down.

"I knew it," she said. "I knew you weren't like other animals."

I am sorry about your camera, he said. He had remorse, a dragon had remorse. How was this possible?

"Um, don't worry about it. Why'd you smash it anyway?"

I'm not supposed to be here, and if those pictures got out, the repercussions would be drastic.

"Oh, well, next time ask. I'll delete them."

I know. I'm sorry. I'll get you a new one.

Aspen giggled, giddy with excitement. "How are you going to do that? You can't exactly waltz into a camera shop."

I have my ways.

Aspen wanted to ask him so many things, to find out how he could talk and why he felt bad about the camera. A talking dragon was far beyond any fantasy she ever had about meeting one.

I am Obsidian.

"I know. I have your name on my ankle. Like you have my name on yours. Why is that?"

I'm afraid that is not a question I can answer right now. But I'm sure you've got others. As I have many questions for you.

"Okay, so what do the words on my ankle mean, aside from your name? Nin Meleth, Nin Aran."

Again, I cannot answer that.

He sounded so familiar, but she couldn't place his voice. And he infuriated her. Why wouldn't he answer her questions about the marking?

"Why can't I take pictures of you? I have pictures of other dragons."

The dragon council closely monitors me. We are not supposed to meddle with humans, and I am far too near to you for the pictures to seem accidental. Plus, I'm not even supposed to be flying anywhere right now.

"Oh," Aspen said, not quite sure how to continue. "But you know dragons are in danger. If I could just get a picture of us together, maybe people will stop thinking dragons are killing people in Yellowstone."

I am aware of that. We are taking steps to prevent it. Dragons are more resourceful than you think. Give us some credit.

Aspen didn't know what to think. Her mind, which was so full of questions a few moments ago, suddenly went blank. "Are you the same dragon I met in South Yellowstone a few months ago?"

Yes, that was me.

"Until I saw you, I'd never seen a black dragon. Are you rare?"

Yes, there is only one black dragon.

"Only one? Why is that?"

Because only the dragon king is black.

Aspen stood, not sure she heard him correctly. "Do you mean to tell me I'm sitting on a hill in Yellowstone having a conversation with the one and only dragon king in the world?"

Yes, that is exactly what I mean.

"Wow, no one is ever going to believe me!" Not only could they talk, but they had a government. A king. And she met him.

Obsidian shifted and brought his face in front of hers. *You must not tell anyone, ANYONE, of our meeting. I am not supposed to be here, and just because I am the dragon king does not mean I have free rein. I am watched more closely than any other dragon, and if word escaped that I was conversing with a human, things would go very badly for me. Do you understand?*

Aspen backed up and put her hands up. "Okay, I get it. No telling anyone."

I need to go. Can we meet again?

"But you just got here. Stay, please, for a little while longer. I want to know more about your government. You're the king. What does that mean? Can you bring another dragon with you? Oh, I met a dragon when I was four. If I tell you about her, can you find her and thank her for me? What do you eat? Why don't you talk to more humans? They might like you more."

Aspen, I'm sorry, not today. I can meet with you tomorrow though.

"No, please, I'm not ready for you go yet." A panic built in her chest. She didn't want to lose this moment.

Tomorrow. I promise.

"I live here in the park. Can we meet near Wraith Falls next time? There is a field on the north side of the falls shielded by trees. You won't be seen, and I will be able to get to you without hiking for an hour."

Of course, I know that area well.

"Wow, okay, bye." Aspen smiled and headed toward the edge of the hill, still not quite sure this was all true. Every few seconds she turned her head to look at him. She paused before he dropped out of sight.

Would you like a ride? Aspen felt him say in her head again.

"A ride?" she asked, confused.

Yes, a ride. I can fly you a lot faster than you can walk.

CHAPTER 21

ASPEN CAME INTO work the next morning beaming. Her hair hung in two long braids, and they swished back and forth when she danced up to the counter.

"Sid, we've got thirty minutes before we open. If you make the mochas, I'll make us bagels, and we can eat before people come in."

Sid blinked. "You want to eat breakfast, with me?"

She shrugged. "Why not?"

"Because you generally try to avoid my presence at all costs."

"Not today." She bounced around the counter and grabbed two bagels.

Her behavior baffled Sid. What was different about today? His stomach flip-flopped. Hopefully, he wouldn't screw this up.

She took the two plates and sat at a four top. Sid took the chair across from her, attempting not to cross any unspoken boundary. Her fingertips brushed his, and he blushed. Aspen jerked, but quickly plastered a smile on her face. It did not reach her eyes. Her hands shook a little as she took a drink of the mocha.

"So, Sid, how did you know about the dragon on the hill? I don't buy the story you told me on our hike." Her voice was sugary sweet.

"I told you I just happened to be hiking out there and saw it."

"That's BS, and you know it." Her mood shifted suddenly. Her happiness was a facade to hide her true intent. But what was it she wanted? She felt nervous and agitated. But not necessarily angry.

"I'm not sure what you are talking about."

"You know something about the dragons, probably more than I do. When you looked at my marking the other night, you didn't seem surprised. And you knew his name was Obsidian. Explain that one."

"That was merely a suggestion. How do you know his name is Obsidian?"

"Because he told me." She crossed her arms across her chest and smiled smugly.

"You were not supposed to tell me that."

She pulled her chair to Sid's side of the table, so close that their knees touched. Sid turned so he could face her. She placed her hands on his legs.

Her faced flushed, and her emotions oozed joy. "And how exactly did you know that?"

"Know what?" Sid had completely forgotten the conversation. His insides were spinning from the placement of her hands and the smell of jasmine that surrounded her.

"That I wasn't supposed to be talking about my conversation with Obsidian. You know. Ha!" She bounced in her seat and stared at Sid expectantly. The disappointment would be brutal.

"Aspen, I'm sorry, but I can't talk about the dragons or Obsidian. And you'd be wise to keep your mouth shut too."

She leaned back in her chair and was silent for a long time, her emotions oscillating from frustration to sadness to anger.

"Do you understand what's going on? The media is going to call for blood. If we don't do anything, dragons are going to die. That doesn't worry you?"

"Of course it does, but I still can't tell you anything."

She threw her hands up. "Seriously. I can fix this dragon problem, but only if you help me."

"You know I really like you, and I want you to keep talking to me, but I can't talk about them."

"Why?"

"Why what?" he asked.

"Why do you like me? What did I ever do to earn your affections? I'm just asking so I can stop doing it, and you'll leave me alone."

Sid grinned, and she gave him a reluctant smile. He moved closer to her. "Because you've got guts, and you like the dragons. No one else has that. Plus, you hate me. That's a challenge too good to pass up."

She didn't smile, but Sid felt her shift from frustration to ease. She leaned forward studying his face. Her bright green eyes stared straight into his, and her hands rested on his chest. He felt a hint of desire, then burning anger.

She shoved him backwards, and he landed hard on the wooden floor. She stood. "You know what, if you won't talk to me about the dragons, I've got nothing to talk to you about. Leave me alone." She grabbed her plate and stalked to the counter.

Desire, anger, fascination, and frustration. Sid had never felt so many of his own emotions at one time. It was exhilarating. He adored her, but she drove him crazy. She hated him as Sid, he knew that. He didn't particularly like it, but at least there was no question where he stood in her eyes.

Aspen met with Obsidian several times over the next week. She even flew on his back a couple of times. They found a new meeting place closer to her house. She got there faster if she drove, but if she needed to, she could hike straight from the house.

At first, it was very awkward between her and Obsidian, but soon meeting with him felt as comfortable as hanging out with Tori.

Sunday night Aspen called goodbye to her parents and made her way out of her house and down the stairs. She opened the door to her jeep, and a horn honked. Sid's Escalade cruised around the corner.

She contemplated chucking a rock at him but thought better of it. She didn't want to see him, let alone talk to him. Sid might have stood a chance with her if he had opened up about the dragons, but he didn't, and he was delusional if he thought anything else would ever happen between them.

Aspen drove down to Wraith Falls and climbed up into the trees that grew thick, and soon silence enveloped her, not even birds sang. The forest seemed endless until she noticed a faint light filtering in above her.

The trees gave way to a setting sun that paled in comparison to the dragon landing fifty yards from her. His great wings collapsed against his body, and the wind whooshed through the trees. He settled on the ground, his head stretching far in front of him.

Hello, Aspen.

She sat next to him and leaned against his chest, feeling the rise and fall of breath. He was quiet for a long time. She waited for him to speak.

Are you in a relationship?

Where did that come from? They should be talking about dragon-human relations, and he asked her about her love life?

"You mean like a boyfriend?"

A relationship, someone who you are close to and attracts you.

"No."

Why?

"I don't know. None of the boys around here are all that interesting."

I can tell when you're lying to me.

"Now there's an interesting conversation topic. How do you know I'm lying?"

I'll answer your questions after you answer mine.

"Fine, but I'm not answering that one." Two could play this game. He refused to answer half her questions.

If you were to be in a relationship, what would you want out of it?

"Spontaneity. Surprise dates, flowers, a walk on the wild side, that sort of thing. Movies and boring dinner dates are out."

But that still doesn't explain why you aren't with anyone.

Obsidian grew quiet. He shifted his head so she was looking him in the face, just staring at her with wide blue eyes under the light of a half moon. He seemed sad somehow, but she didn't feel right asking him about it. Maybe he'd just gotten out of a bad relationship. Aspen supposed now would not be an appropriate time to ask about dragon love, but Obsidian had piqued her curiosity.

She didn't know why she told him so much. She'd never confided her secret desires to anyone before. It was hard for her to even think about relationships after Marc. She dated occasionally, but no one ever really sparked her interest. Of course, most of those dates consisted of bad movies and Olive Garden.

CHAPTER 22

OVER THE NEXT two weeks, Sid spent nearly every waking moment with Aspen. Of course, she didn't realize who he was, but he was trying to find a way to tell her. He was afraid she'd hate him once she found out the truth.

Sid drove along the familiar tree-lined path into the park. It was much easier to change form in the trees of Yellowstone than his backyard. He was about ten miles into the park when he saw Aspen walking on the side of the road. He pulled up beside her and rolled down the window.

"Aspen, what are you doing?"

"What does it look like I'm doing? I'm walking." She sped up a little and pulled her jacket closer to her neck.

"Well, do you want a ride?"

"No, I don't. I'm just fine, thanks." She crossed to the other side of the street and continued, hugging the pines.

Sid pulled the car off the road and got out. "Okay, then I'll come with you."

"That's really not necessary." Aspen zipped up her jacket and marched on.

Sid deliberated for only a moment and then ran to catch up with her. He could feel her frustration. "Why are you walking anyway?"

She stopped for a second and leaned up against a tall cedar. "My car broke down."

"Why didn't you call someone?"

"My mom and dad aren't allowed to have cell phones at work. Tori's up in Livingston, and Ella's phone is turned off. After I tried them, my phone died. It's not that far to my house."

"Isn't it lucky that your prince charming came to rescue you?"

Her expression froze. "You're not my prince charming. You're Tori's, but not mine."

"Except that I don't want Tori. I want you." Sid smiled at her in a way he thought would be encouraging. Or maybe not. She glared at him and kept going.

He followed.

"You know," she said. "I'm really getting sick of having these conversations with you. Sid, you hardly know me. How could you possibly know you'd be good for me?"

An abrupt wind blew through the trees and sent pine needles flying. Sid ignored the question. "Why don't we play a game? We have a long walk ahead of us, and we might as well entertain ourselves."

"You don't have to stay with me. I can go by myself."

Sid stayed silent.

Finally, she spoke. "Fine, what's the game?"

"Let's pretend I'm your boyfriend."

"In your dreams." She laughed. Her laughter was forced, short.

"Quite frequently."

She crossed her arms and stalked away. She was so angry. Sid, on the other hand, was having the time of his life. Even in her irritation, she was beautiful and entertaining. Sid could tell he was bugging the hell out of her, but he hadn't gone too far. Yet.

He stepped over the milepost and stood close behind her. "Pick a day and a time, and I will tell you what we'd be doing, if I was your boyfriend." At her fierce look he amended, "Unless, of course, you want to decide what we'd be doing."

"This is the stupidest thing I've ever heard of. You're not my boyfriend, nor will you ever be my boyfriend. Give it up."

Not likely. Perhaps he should try a different avenue.

"Can you explain why you hate me so much? What did I ever do to you?"

"I don't hate you. But I could never love you. You look too much like—" She paused.

"Like who?"

She stopped and looked him straight in the eyes, something she rarely did. The depth of pain was enough to make him wish he could go back in her past and erase whatever caused it.

"Like who?" Sid repeated.

She shook her head. "Never mind, we'll play your stupid game."

He stumbled over a root in the ground, shocked that she actually agreed. "Okay, pick a day and a time, and I'll tell you what we'd be doing if I were your boyfriend."

She rolled her eyes. "Are you for real? That's your game? Dumbest thing I've ever heard of."

Sid waited and didn't respond. After a few minutes she threw her arms up. "Fine, Wednesday after school."

"Easy, doing homework in your room."

"Boring." She kicked at a stone on the ground.

"I wasn't done. After that, we would go for a drive."

"To where?" she asked.

"Who knows? Wherever the road takes us. We would flip a coin at every intersection, heads we turn right, tails we turn left, and if we can't find a penny we would just go straight. We might end up at a funky roadside diner, or we might end up in Gardiner. The fun part is the journey. Pick another one."

Jackpot. Her anger disappeared, replaced with confusion. She continued walking.

"Tuesday night," she said, attempting to hide her smile. It was startling, feeling her happy around him for once.

"Playing games with your family. I kick butt at Cranium."

She stopped and looked at him. "How did you—"

"Pick another one." He stepped closer to her.

She watched her own fingers as they fiddled with her zipper. "Saturday."

On the second step to Aspen, Sid decided to make his move. "On Saturday morning, you would wake up to find a yellow rose and a note on your pillow. The note tells you to go to the beginning of the trail to Heart Lake."

Aspen still didn't face him, but she didn't back away either. Sid took another step toward her. "Once there you will find a backpack with a locked zipper and another note with directions to the next clue."

Aspen looked up and blinked, surprised to find Sid's face only six inches from hers. Sid hesitated, afraid she might move away. Her eyes were huge, the long dark lashes reaching up into her eyebrows. He continued. "Eventually, you'll find me, probably around noon. We'll have a picnic and continue the hike together."

"The backpack," she whispered, so close he could see the faint line of freckles across her nose. "What's in the backpack?"

"I can't tell you. It would ruin the surprise," Sid said.

He didn't register her movement. Frantic lips met his, and hands twisted in his hair. At first, Sid didn't move. His brain raced to comprehend, then he understood. This was the moment he'd been longing for, fantasizing about since the day he sealed himself to her.

He placed his arms around her waist and pulled her close. Aspen's hands relaxed and rested on the back of his neck. Her heart beat rapidly against his. His head exploded, and he tuned out everything else. The movement of their lips was not enough. He desired, no he needed to taste her lips. He tentatively licked the outer edge of her lip. Watermelon. She gasped. Her tongue met his, and the urgency began over again. Wow.

CHAPTER 23

A CAR RACED PAST and honked the horn. Aspen moved her hands to Sid's chest and pushed. He stumbled, confused at what had happened. Her face twisted in revulsion, and Sid tried to read her feelings—he picked up horror and disgust as she ran from him. They were less than a quarter mile from her home, so he let her go.

Aspen was intentionally rude to him ninety-five percent of the time. Usually it didn't bother him. He knew she didn't like him, and for the most part, the things she said and did only encouraged him. The revulsion on her face and the disgust she felt were too much though. He waited until she was out of sight and then transformed, taking out a large pine tree. He took off and flew in the opposite direction of where they were supposed to meet.

Sid didn't know why she kissed him. He did know that it was the highlight of his life. Better than learning to fly, better than meeting Skye, better than even the moment he fell in love with Aspen. It was an experience he hoped to repeat many times, but that was obviously not happening. Because although it was the best moment of his life, it was apparently one of her worst. Why was she so repulsed by him?

In his confusion, he had not paid attention to where he was going. The snow-capped Eagle's Peak greeted him. Home. The place where he should reign as king, but instead would meet his death. He wanted to turn himself in, accept his punishment, and leave this world; instead, he turned and flew toward their meeting place. He needed to find out why she despised Sid. He was a dragon. He'd hold her down if he had to. She would not leave until she told him.

Aspen was already in the clearing when Sid arrived. He hovered for a few moments observing her. Part of him did not want to see her. He wanted to remain in the air, treasure the kiss, and not pursue the wound. But he didn't. His talons dug deep into the earth when he landed. Aspen sat near a tree, eyes closed. Even his landing did not trigger a response.

"I kissed Sid," she mumbled.

Sid wasn't sure he heard her correctly. *What did you say?*

She opened her eyes and looked up at him. "I kissed Sid."

He was not expecting her to bring it up right away.

Who is Sid?

"Sid is this horrid boy from school who likes me."

If he's so horrid, then why did you kiss him?

"I didn't mean that. I do actually like him. He just brings up bad memories. That's beside the point. I'm so confused." She stood and walked in circles in front of him.

Keep talking, maybe you'll figure it out, and if you don't, maybe I can help.

She stopped, glared up at him, and said, "You never did tell me what that mark meant on my ankle, but I think I've figured it out."

What does that have to do with you kissing Sid?

"I'll get there in a minute. First I need you to understand something."

Okay.

"You understand the mechanics of kissing, right?"

Lips, tongue, desire. Yes, I have a good understanding of it.

"Do dragons have an equivalent of kissing?"

I don't believe so. Physical relations are not the same for us. Our relationships are primarily mental and emotional, except when we mate.

"And how does that work? Dragon mating?"

Sid sighed. *That is off topic. You were explaining about this kiss.*

"Fine. Most of the time when people kiss, they close their eyes. I don't know why we do that. While I was kissing Sid, I didn't picture his face in my head."

She stopped pacing and curled her hands into fists, squeezing her eyes shut. Anger burst forth like flames. For a minute Sid thought perhaps she would throw a temper tantrum like a few of the toddlers who came into the Purple Dragon. Instead, she sat and pulled her knees to her chest.

Sid was confused. This was not the conversation he imagined having with her. *So who did you picture in your head?*

She remained in a ball and talked to her knees. "Obsidian, I saw your face. That mark, it means I'm in love with you, doesn't it? How did this happen? I'm so messed up. I just kissed a boy I can't even look at, and all I thought about was a stinking dragon, no offense or anything." She paused. "This is so wrong. From the day I first saw you, I couldn't stop thinking about you."

Sid understood now. She believed she was in love with a beast, not a man. She was disgusted with herself. This would be the best time to explain everything. Tell her exactly who he was and what it all meant. But no. He did what any self-respecting male did when a female needed reassurance. He lied.

First off, that mark doesn't necessarily have anything to do with romantic love. It means we are sealed together, but that could have a number of different meanings. And second, I wouldn't worry about seeing my face when you kissed him. Maybe it's because our voices sound the same to you. It could be that you just associate us together.

"You know what? I heard him, in my head, like I hear you. I could hear his thoughts. He sounded just like you. Maybe you're right."

What do you mean you "heard" him?

"I could hear him. I didn't really pay attention. I think I've gotten too used to hearing you. It was fuzzy. I would catch an occasional thought. Things like 'been waiting for this,' 'watermelon,' and 'wow.'" She smiled briefly and then frowned again.

She should not have been able to hear his thoughts. He'd been diligent about protecting them. Maybe this had to do with the whole sealed thing. He wondered who he could ask without arousing suspicions.

That is highly unusual but would explain why you saw my face when you were kissing him.

He needed to tell her. It would make this easier for her. But then she'd be angry with him for not telling her earlier and for lying. *There is something you should know.*

"Can it wait? I really need to make sure this whole kiss thing doesn't get back to Tori. I'll see you tomorrow?"

Of course.

Sid flew away as soon as she was out of sight. He had to get home if she was planning on talking to him.

Sid's phone rang as he walked into the house. He sat on the counter and answered it.

"Hey," Aspen said.

"That kiss must've been better than I thought. You've never called me before." He grinned, pleased with himself.

"Yeah, about that. This is all a mistake. I'm sorry. I shouldn't have kissed you. No one can find out. Ever."

"I'm not crazy about keeping our relationship a secret, but for you, I'd do just about anything."

Aspen sighed. "No, Sid, I don't think you understand. We can't be together. Even in secret."

His stomach tensed. "I don't understand."

"I don't like you like that. I got caught up in the moment, but it didn't mean anything. Please. Can we just forget this happened?"

Sid leaned against the cupboard and thought.

"Why?"

"Why what?"

"Why can't we be together?"

"There are a thousand reasons. Tori's totally in love with you. She's my best friend, and there's no way I'd betray her like this."

"We can work through that. It might take some time, but if we can find someone else for Tori to love, then we'll be fine. I can be patient."

"That's not the only reason."

"Give me your best one. I bet I can talk you out of it."

"This isn't fair. Please just promise me you won't say anything. It would devastate Tori."

Sid thought for a minute. He could win her over, but only if she opened up to him.

"Okay. I won't say anything, but only under one condition."

"There's always something with you."

"Wait. Two conditions."

She sighed again. He could almost see her beautiful exasperated face. "Fine. Two conditions. Tell me how I'm going to sell my soul."

He frowned. "One, you have to be my friend. No more ice queen from you."

"Friends only. You can't go all lovey dovey on me."

"You doubt my ability to be your friend?"

"You did kiss me today."

"Nope, you kissed me."

She didn't respond. He loved this. She might have put him off, but it wouldn't last long.

After a few seconds she spoke. "What's the second condition?"

"You have to tell me the number one reason why we can't be together. It's not because of Tori."

"How do you always do this to me?"

"Do what?"

"Get me to tell you things I shouldn't tell anyone."

He took a chance. "Because you love me?"

"You know, it might be easier if that was the case. But see, Sid, that's the problem. I'm in love with someone else."

She hung up the phone before he could respond. Sid's chest burned with jealousy. Who the hell could she be in love with?

He hopped off the counter and paced the kitchen. He replayed the whole afternoon in his head, searching for clues. From the moment he saw her walking on the side of the road to her spilling her guts to him as Obsidian.

He froze. That was it.

She wasn't in love with anyone else at all.

She was in love with Obsidian. Which he knew, but he just thought she was talking about some other guy. He was so relieved.

He had to tell her.

CHAPTER 24

ASPEN WAS SO in for it. She had no idea how she was going to be friends with Sid. All he had to do was a throw a little romance at her, and she would lock lips with him. She smiled at the memory and then scowled. She didn't like him. Not really, but he was like Obsidian personified, and that made it hard for her to not like him. Until Obsidian said it, she'd never made the connection, but their personalities were similar, and Obsidian's voice sounded just like Sid's. She wondered how they were connected. Sid was involved with the dragons, but she didn't know how.

If she were friends with him, maybe she could figure it out. She was trying to find the positive in all of this and wondering how Tori would take it. Nothing about this would be easy. If Aspen were to suddenly start talking to Sid, Tori would get suspicious. No, she had to take this slow. Warm up to him little by little so Tori didn't get jealous.

She heard the front door open, and she bounded downstairs. Her mom and dad stood in the doorway looking worried.

"Everything okay?" Aspen asked.

"Yeah," her dad answered. "But we're not any closer to finding the animal that killed Matt and the hiker. The media is starting to make a fuss. We put a few restrictions on hiking, but that doesn't matter because Matt was killed right off the road."

He set his hat on the table and sank into a chair. "Where's your car?"

"Broke down about a half a mile back."

"How'd you get home?"

"I walked."

Her mom gasped. "Aspen, you can't be out walking. It's not safe."

"I was fine. I'm being safe. I'm only hiking in the area around our house."

Stacey sat on the chair next to Aspen and patted her hand. "I know. I just worry. We've had deaths before, but these have me rattled. What are we going to do about your car?"

"I'll take them to school tomorrow," Jason said. "We'll leave a little early and tow your car to the shop. If it's something easy, you can get it after school. Tori can take you to pick it up."

Aspen and her dad spent a little too long in the shop, and she missed homeroom altogether, which meant she didn't have to talk to Sid until algebra. She was having second thoughts about the whole arrangement. She couldn't even think about him without remembering how his lips felt on hers. She frowned as she slipped into biology a few minutes late. Thankfully, the class had a substitute, and he'd already started a movie. That meant Aspen could check out.

She set her notebook down and stared at the screen absentmindedly. Sid's gorgeous face filled her imagination. She didn't want to think about those captivating eyes. What if she forgot she wasn't supposed to like him and kissed him again? Tori would kill her. Besides, she was in love with Obsidian. At least that's what she kept trying to tell herself. Every time her mind wandered, she thought of Sid.

The bell rang all too soon, and Aspen met Tori at her locker.

"Where were you this morning?"

"We had to drop my car off at the shop. Can you bring me by after school to pick it up?"

"Sure." Tori tossed her blonde hair over her shoulder. "So, I'm thinking of making my move at lunch."

"What move?"

"On Sid. I'm going to ask him to go see a movie with me this weekend. I'm super nervous, but I think he'll say yes. He's been talking to me a lot."

"Are you sure? Maybe he was just being nice."

"Whose side on are you on anyway? You know when someone says something like that, you're supposed to say, 'of course he'll say yes.'"

"I just don't want you to get hurt."

"Whatever. I'll see you at lunch."

She hadn't even talked to Sid yet, and already she'd pissed Tori off. Aspen knew Sid would say no and Tori would whine about it. Aspen hoped she wouldn't slip and say, "told you so."

Aspen took her seat in front of Sid and didn't look back at him. She was supposed to be his friend but didn't know how to do that. She got out her notebook so it looked like she was doing something productive. Sid shifted in his seat behind her. Hopefully, he wouldn't try to talk to her.

It felt like someone was pulling on her hair, but she didn't want to give Sid the satisfaction of getting her attention, so she ignored the occasional tugs throughout class. Just before the bell rang, her hair fell to her shoulders. Dammit. He'd taken out her bun. He chuckled behind her. She turned and gathered up the sticks she used to put her hair up and glared at him without saying anything. Then escaped from the room. The problem with Sid was that she couldn't be neutral about him. She either hated him or loved him.

CHAPTER 25

A T LUNCH SID sat next to Tori and across from Aspen. He waited for her to talk to him, since she promised she'd be his friend. Instead, she carried on a conversation with Tori and acted like he wasn't there. Her inattentiveness annoyed him. Tori, however, had scooted closer to him and set her hand on his knee. He had to get out of there. He stood and Tori grabbed his hand.

"Where are you going?"

He didn't look at her but instead, at Aspen. She brushed her hair over her shoulder and stared at a tree across the courtyard. Sid felt a wave possessiveness he didn't know was possible. She was finally his and acted like nothing ever happened. He suddenly had the overwhelming desire to kiss her. He had to have her. Right now.

He climbed up onto the table and took her face in his hands. Her eyes opened wide. He pushed his mouth against hers, and she responded instantly, her hands gripping the front of his T-shirt. In that moment, there was nothing gentle or loving about his kiss. He claimed what was his. Tori be damned. Aspen stood and leaned into him. A chair pushed him sideways, and he broke away from Aspen. Tori ran for the doors.

"Asshole," Aspen said and took off after Tori.

CHAPTER 26

BATHROOM. SHE'D RUN for the bathroom. Aspen felt like the suckiest best friend ever. Why did Sid have to kiss her, and why did she have to react? Tori would never speak to her again. Aspen pushed open the door, and after checking each stall, she decided Tori must've gone home. Aspen slid out the bathroom door and was nearly to the main doors when Mr. VanDyke stepped out of his office.

"Aspen, where are you going?"

She looked down, avoiding his gaze. "Home."

"Just because you're a senior doesn't give you the right to come and go as you please. You will head to class, or I will call your parents."

Aspen couldn't explain her need to leave to him and narc on Tori. Tori's anger wouldn't change much in the next few hours, and Aspen's parents were already starting to crack down on her freedoms because of the deaths. No reason to add Mr. VanDyke into the mix.

After school, Dan took Aspen to get her car. Then she drove to Tori's house, but her car wasn't in the driveway. Aspen tried the Purple Dragon too, but Tori's bright green beetle wasn't there either. She drove around town for a while, checking in with other friends, but no one had seen Tori.

As evening approached, Aspen found herself driving down the long driveway to Sid's house. After lunch, she successfully avoided him for the rest of the day. Her anger had died, but she still had no idea where this relationship was going. Sid wasn't worth her friendship with Tori, but Aspen didn't know if that was salvageable anymore.

She knocked on the door. Theo answered, looking grumpy. Ella must be at work.

"Is Sid here?" Aspen asked.

"Yeah, I think he's sleeping. You can go on up."

Aspen started up the stairs.

"Wait," he said. He still stood with his hand on the door handle. "I hope you won't take this the wrong way or anything, but it'd be a really bad idea for you to pursue things with Sid."

"Why?"

"Sid was not sent to Gardiner to find a girlfriend."

"What's that supposed to mean?"

"He's not allowed to see you, romantically speaking."

"I think Sid is old enough to make that decision on his own. I don't answer to you. If you don't want me going out with Sid, you'll have to approach him on it, not me."

He sighed. "Okay, but when you are asked, I did my duty and told you to stay away from him."

Aspen didn't expect him to back down so easily. And what he said was a bit mental. She might have to break it to Ella that her man was a little off his rocker. Besides, Sid was the one who came after her, not the other way around. Why would Theo bother her with a warning like that?

All the doors on the second floor were open except one. He was face down on his bed fast asleep. She sat next to him and traced his bare shoulder blades with her finger, surprised at her need to touch him. Everything about Sid surprised her. She moved his long hair away from his face so she could see him.

A twinge a fear crept in as she looked at his peaceful face. He looked so much like Marc that it was unnerving. Lately, when Sid was talking, she could easily tell the difference, but here he looked too much like the nightmare she remembered.

She turned to check out the rest of his room. Hanging above his computer was a picture of the silver dragon she had taken that day at school. He must've gotten a print from Ella.

Next to his computer was a large bookshelf. There was the usual collection of boy books on the shelves, Stephen King, Michael Creighton, J.R.R. Tolkien, Christopher Paolini, and even Harry Potter. He also had several books that did not belong in a teenager's room, books about politics, world governments, and the UN. And then there was a shelf full of books in a completely different language. It looked like nothing she had ever seen before.

"Aspen?" asked a confused voice.

She turned, and he was sitting up on his bed. She sank into the chair at his computer desk. He needed to put a shirt on, or she was going to pass out.

"Hi," Aspen said meekly. Now that he was awake, she wasn't sure what to say. She couldn't remember why she'd come in the first place.

"What are you doing here?"

"I'm sorry," Aspen replied. "I'll go." She stood and walked to the door.

"No, wait," he said, coming after her. He grabbed her hand and turned her around. She became acutely aware he was only wearing boxer shorts. She couldn't help herself and peeked. SpongeBob. She snickered and forced herself to look him in the face.

"I thought you were furious with me. I'm sorry I kissed you at school today. I wasn't thinking clearly. Not that I ever think clearly in your presence."

Aspen blushed. "No, I'm not mad. I was, but I got over it."

He raised his eyebrows, and his blue eyes bore into hers. The gaze was too intense so she looked down, which was even worse. His bare chest was begging to be touched. She took a step back.

"Can you put some clothes on?"

His face colored.

"I'm sorry. Am I making you uncomfortable?"

"Not exactly, but I'll be more coherent if I don't have to keep reminding myself to look you in the eyes."

He dug into a pile of clothes on the floor. Aspen sat on the edge of the bed. At first, she tried not to stare at him, but then gave it up as a lost cause. Every time he moved, another muscle flexed. Aspen couldn't identify a single fleshy part on his body.

"Do you work out a lot?" As she asked, she realized she knew very little about him. She spent so much time in the last several weeks trying to avoid him that she didn't take any time to learn about his family life or what he enjoyed. She liked him, but this whole relationship could be over before it began if they had nothing in common.

"Um, yeah. Theo and I are pretty competitive with each another. We have an entire personal gym in the basement," he said as he buttoned his jeans. He pulled a wrinkled green T-shirt over his head, and his hair flew in a million different directions. He tried to smooth it down, but that only made it worse. He sat next to her and took her hand in his own.

"Is this okay?" he asked.

She nodded, not trusting herself to talk. He rubbed the back of her hand with his thumb, and she looked at him. He moved her hair out of her face with the other hand, leaned in, and gently kissed her lips. She was disappointed when he pulled away quickly.

"Am I allowed to kiss you now?"

"I guess." She thought the next thing he would ask would be about who she was in love with, and she had no idea how to explain that.

"You still haven't answered my question. Why are you here? Don't get me wrong, I'm very glad you are. But, Aspen, you never do anything without a purpose, and I'm sure you had a better reason than to stare at my half-naked body."

Aspen smiled at him. She was surprised he had managed to learn so much about her in the last few weeks. Normally, she didn't do anything unless there was a good reason. "Honestly, I don't know. I was trying to find Tori, and I ended up here."

"Well, then, I suppose you should probably finish the search. You won't be happy with me until you've settled things with her. Once you decide it's okay to be with me, I'll be here." He got up and opened the door. He was right, but that didn't change the fact his words stung. Aspen managed to make it out to her car before crying.

She hadn't expected to feel so upset by his rejection, and she didn't know how to make things right with Tori.

Aspen's hands shook as she turned the key. The engine clicked but would not roar. She groaned and tried again. Nothing. Sucking up her pride, she found an old balled up napkin and dried her face. Then she knocked on the door again. Sid answered, looking confused.

"My car won't start. Can you take me home?"

He nodded, reached for her and intertwined their fingers, as he brought their hands to his lips. He kissed the back of her hand. "I'm sorry. I didn't mean to be cruel. I'm frustrated we can't be together in public yet."

Aspen shrugged, still not quite sure how to handle what was going on.

He took her home, and they sat in the driveway for a few minutes. Sid leaned over and kissed her again. It took every ounce of self-discipline she had to drag herself away and out of his car. She shut the front door and stood there for a minute. Sid absolutely took her into another world. She wasn't sure if she could get used to being with him all the time.

"That's not Tori's car," Stacey said.

Oops. Aspen didn't say anything. She forgot that she had texted her mom and told her that her car busted again, and Tori was bringing her home.

"Are you going to explain?" Stacey asked.

No good story occurred to her, so she told her the truth.

"That was Sid's car."

"Isn't he the new boy? The one you work with? The one you told me you absolutely loathed? The one that Tori's been going on about?"

"Yeah, that's him."

Her mom deliberated for a moment. Aspen could tell she was confused, but she didn't want to give her any more information than needed.

"Explain."

She may as well get used to the idea. "Sid's my new boyfriend." Aspen left her at the door and went upstairs to her room.

Tori was sprawled out on Aspen's bed when she entered the room. That explained the ambush from her mother.

"When were you going to bother telling me?" she asked, sitting up. "About Sid?"

"Yeah." She crossed her arms and blinked rapidly. Probably trying to keep the tears away, but a few escaped anyway.

"Tonight, actually. I've been out all afternoon looking for you." Aspen took off her jacket and sat next to Tori.

"Sure, and that's why you were making out with him in the car a few minutes ago?" She moved away.

"I'm so sorry. This wasn't planned. It just happened. I didn't go after him, I swear. He came after me. In spite of all my efforts to stay away from him, he managed to win me over. But he's not worth losing you. Tell me what I can do to fix this, and I'll do it."

Tori got up and walked to the other side of the room. "It's too late. There's absolutely nothing you can do. But I hope every time you kiss him you remember the price you paid for his affection."

She slammed the door behind her.

Aspen sighed and lay on her bed, her head reeling. So much had happened over the last couple of days, and Aspen wasn't sure if she could take it all in. On the down side, Tori wouldn't be speaking to her, but on the up side, Aspen had Sid. Two days ago that would have been a bad thing. Strange how things change. Someone knocked on the door. Oh jeez, what now?

"Come in," Aspen called.

Rowan opened the door and sat at her desk.

"Thanks for blowing my chances with Tori."

"Seriously, Rowan? I had a really long day, and if you came in here to yell at me about ruining your chances with a girl you never had a chance with, please leave."

"Actually, I came to tell you that I saw you."

"Saw me what? Make out with Sid? Mom saw me too, so no surprises there." Aspen rubbed her neck. The muscles had stiffened.

"No, I didn't see that, and I don't want to, so keep the PDAs down. I saw you with the dragon."

"What dragon?" Aspen asked through clenched teeth.

"The big black one."

Could this week get any worse? Tori would never speak to her again, her car busted, she was probably grounded, and now her dragon-hating twin saw her with Obsidian.

"How did you do that?"

"I followed you."

"Why? You barely leave your room."

He twisted his hands. "I'm still trying to work through my anxieties."

Aspen had to admit she was impressed. She didn't realize he had it in him. But now she had a problem.

"What are you going to do about it?" Aspen asked.

He sat on her bed. "What do you mean?"

"Well, my anti-dragon sibling, this cannot be a good thing for you. What are you going to do about the fact your sister is now 'in league' with them?" She knew she was being unreasonable, but her head was starting to hurt, and she couldn't think straight.

"I'm not Tori. I just wanted to know what's going on. And I'm not anti-dragon, I'm just scared of them, that's all."

"You're scared of everything."

"I know you've had a crappy day. You don't need to take it out on me."

"Crappy? Rowan, this could quite possibly be the worst week of my life."

"Worse even than the time you went rock climbing alone and got stranded on the face of the mountain?"

"Yeah, worse than that."

He lay next to her and propped his head in his hand. "How could this be the worse week ever? You made out with Sid. Something I know you've wanted to do for a while."

Aspen shoved him on the shoulder. "That's so not true. What makes you think that?"

"Oh please. I see the way you look at him at school."

"Whatever. Anyway, my car broke down twice, and Tori is pissed. I made out with a fabulous boy, and I have no one to talk to."

"You have me, plus I know about the dragon, which I'm sure you've been dying to tell someone. Seeing as how it's not a New York Times article yet, you didn't tell Tori. You've only been on friendly terms with Sid for..." he said, looking at his watch. "Three hours now. I don't think you told anyone about him. Why?"

Aspen looked at her brother for few minutes before answering. They had never been close. Their sister snatched Aspen from the crib as soon as she could. She didn't pay attention to Rowan; he was a boy. So even though they were twins, Aspen was closer to her older sister than him. Plus, they were complete opposites. Aspen was the daredevil, and he was the chicken. She feared for his kids; they would literally have to wear a plastic bubble when they left the house.

In spite of that, she trusted him. If she could tell anyone about Obsidian, it would be Rowan. He was loyal to their family, and she knew he would never betray her. Besides, even though she had Sid and their newfound relationship, he was still mum on the dragons.

"Obsidian asked me not to tell anyone. He's not supposed to be around humans. In fact, I got the impression he's not supposed to be out at all."

Rowan sat up quickly. "You mean they can talk?"

"Yeah, except not with their mouths. They talk with their minds."

Rowan scowled and started to get up. "You know, Aspen, I thought things were finally getting to be cool between us. I can't believe you'd try to trick me like this."

Aspen grabbed his arm. "I'm telling the truth. They talk with their minds. It's amazing."

He looked at her for a minute. "Fine, I believe you. Well, not really, but prove it."

"How?"

"I want to come with you the next time you go see him."

Aspen laughed out loud. Her brother was the most timid person she knew, and he wanted to meet the dragon she hung out with. "Are you serious? You'll pee your pants."

He chuckled. "Yeah, probably, but don't you think it's time I grew up? The fear I feel half the time is paralyzing. Sometimes I even struggle walking out the front door. I'm seventeen years old and don't even have my driver's license because I'm scared of everything. I need to get over my fear. I figure by facing the thing that scares me the most, I'll be able to approach the rest of my life easier."

Aspen couldn't believe he was confiding in her, so she chose her words carefully. "Don't you think therapy may be a better option? I'm afraid of what this kind of trauma might do to you."

"No, this is the best way. You trust the dragon, and I trust you. It should be cake."

"Well, I'll need to talk to him first. He's not too keen on people knowing about him. The first time I met him, before I knew he could talk, he smashed my camera."

"What did you do?"

"I called him an idiot."

Rowan gaped. "You insulted a fully grown dragon before you knew he was nice? How could you be so stupid?"

"I think I was born without fear genes. That was the first time he spoke to me."

"Did he say 'cut it out I'll incinerate you?'"

Aspen laughed. "No, he asked if I wanted a ride."

Aspen watched Rowan's expression, and sure enough he looked dumbstruck.

CHAPTER 27

S ID WAS NERVOUS picking Aspen up the next morning. Her moods shifted quickly, and he was afraid she had gone back to hating him. When she slid into the car, she kissed him full on the lips. He tried to prolong the kiss, but she pulled away. "Do you mind giving my brother a ride? I usually take him to school."

He looked out the window and saw Rowan pacing on the porch. Did he actually think Sid would say no?

"Sure thing," Sid said. He moved his books around in the backseat. Aspen waved Rowan to the car. He got in and looked around warily. As usual with Rowan, Sid could feel his intense fear. It was nearly crippling. Interesting because it never showed on his face. "Are you okay?" Sid asked him.

"I'm fine," he said and leaned down to pull up his socks.

Sid turned around and still felt that debilitating fear. "Are you sure? I get the impression you're afraid of something. I'm not that bad of a driver."

"I'm fi—"

"Rowan is scared of everything. We think there's a name for it, but he won't talk to a shrink. He's probably scared we're going to kiss in front of him or something. He'll be fine. Let's go."

Aspen's bluntness shocked Sid. If Pearl had done likewise, he'd be very angry. Rowan didn't get upset, and his fear subsided slightly.

Sid tried to make small talk as they drove to school, but he couldn't get much out of Rowan. Sid made a mental note to learn more about those video games Rowan played so he could talk to him next time.

Aspen held his hand as they drove, but the closer they got to school, the more he felt her own anxiety rise.

"Are you okay?" he asked her.

"What are you, some kind of psychic or something?" she asked.

"No, you have a death grip on my hand."

"Oh, well, uh."

Rowan spoke up. "Tori's pissed at her because she's going out with you. She's terrified Tori's never going to speak to her again."

Sid wondered if it was normal for twins to answer for each other like that.

CHAPTER 28

THAT AFTERNOON SID convinced Aspen to do homework with him. Which actually consisted of her lying on his bed trying to decipher his dragon books and him doing her homework for her.

"What language is this?"

Sid looked up; she had the book upside down. "Can't tell you that."

She pouted. "This whole secret thing is going to end us eventually."

"I hate it when you say things like that."

"It's true." She slammed the book down on the bed. "You know how I feel about the dragons, and yet you won't say a word about them, even though I know you're connected to them somehow. Besides, if you tell me, maybe we could stop the witch-hunt that is beginning."

He sighed. Maybe he should just tell her. Now was as good of time as any. Would she be angry or pleased? There was no in between with Aspen. It would be one or the other.

He sat next to her on the bed and brushed her hair over her shoulder.

"Stop trying to distract me."

He grinned and leaned down and kissed her neck. She shivered.

"I mean it, Sid. I want answers."

He pulled her into his lap and looked deep into her eyes. Those gorgeous green things would be the death of him yet. He started to speak when her lips met his, and Sid forgot all about telling her.

A half hour later Sid lay on his bed half asleep with Aspen lying on his chest. If he could distract her like that every time she asked questions, he might never have to tell her the truth.

Aspen's phone buzzed, and she looked at the screen. She scrolled through a text, sent something back, and scrambled off him.

"Let's go."

Twenty minutes later they stopped at a small yellow house on the outskirts of town. Weeds grew in flowerbeds, and yellow dandelions dotted the overgrown yard. Ella flung the door open before Aspen even knocked. "I knew you'd come. Sid's gonna love this. I've got a few phone calls to make. You'll be okay?"

"We'll be fine. How's the mother?" Aspen asked.

"Recovering. Don't approach her. She's grumpy."

Aspen laughed. "Okay, do you need me to take one home?"

"No, I don't think your mom has forgiven me for the last time. They'll be fine here."

Aspen grabbed Sid's hand and dragged him through the living room and into the kitchen. The linoleum had holes in it, and the tiny table in the corner had a phonebook under one leg to keep it balanced. A few dishes sat in the sink.

They headed down a flight of stairs to the basement, although the basement looked more like a hospital. It was brightly lit with sterile white walls and stainless steel tables. Two large cages took up the back half of the space. In one there was a giant grizzly bear with bandages around her head. Two small cubs fought over an odd looking toy in the other cage. Aspen opened the second cage, scooped up one of the cubs, and thrust him into Sid's arms. She gathered up the other cub and walked out. Sid followed, the bear squirming in his arms and gnawing on his hands.

Calm down, little one. I won't hurt you, Sid said.

The cub immediately stopped moving. *I'm sorry, Master Dragon. I didn't recognize you.*

No worries. What's your name?

I'm Black and my sister is Berry. My mother is Oakley. What's your name?

I am Obsidian.

His eyes widened. *The new dragon king?*

Yes, I'm surprised news has spread that quickly.

The birds, they tell everyone. What are you doing like this?

You mean as a human?

Yeah, humans are gross. Why would you want to be one of them?

It is something all royal dragons must do. We need to learn to maintain communication with them. Very few humans know we can do this.

Oh, he seemed disappointed. He probably imagined a much grander reason.

"Sid, is your bear okay?" Aspen asked.

Sid looked up at her, surprised. He had gotten so wrapped up in his conversation he forgot she was there. "Yes," he said and put Black down. He scampered over to his mother's cage.

"It was just strange. He wasn't moving."

She sat on the floor with Berry cradled in her lap. The bear was sucking vigorously on a bottle. "There's another bottle on the table. You can feed the other cub."

Sid was reaching for the bottle when Black spoke up. *Mama says I'm not allowed to be fed by you. She said it would be a disgrace for a dragon to have to feed a bear. I'll wait for the girl.*

You have to prove to her that you won't. She expects me to feed you.

And you, the dragon king, answer to her?

He laughed. *Yes, I do.*

He walked over to Black, picked him up, and settled next to Aspen. Obedient to his mother's instructions, Black refused the bottle. "He won't take it from me. Maybe you should try."

"Huh, that seems weird. I wonder if there is something wrong with him."

Black told Berry who Sid was, and she trembled when Aspen handed her to him. *Your brother told me you were Berry.*

Yes.

And how did you end up down here?

I don't know. A car I think.

You don't have to be afraid of me.

I know, but I've never met a dragon before, and you are the king. I can't wait to tell everyone I met you.

They played with the cubs for a while. Before they left, Sid approached the mother. He knelt in front of her cage. She shook with anxiety at meeting him.

You have very brave children.

Thank you, Your Majesty.

Be nice to the humans who are taking care of you. They'll get you patched up and home before you know it.

Yes, Your Majesty.

"How did you get involved with the bears?" Sid asked Aspen on the way home.

"Has Ella ever told you her story?"

"Nope."

"Do you even know how old she is?"

"Nope, but I don't see what this has to do with bears."

"She's thirty-two."

"No way."

"Yeah, she doesn't look her age at all. Anyway, she ran off to California when she turned eighteen and went a little crazy. A few years later she met a guy named Jeremy. Then her parents died, and so she came home, but not before making a detour to Vegas and getting married. She took over the coffee shop, and Jeremy always had a thing for bears, so he started a sanctuary.

"I went to the sanctuary for a school field trip in seventh grade. I already had a penchant for danger, so instead of getting back on the bus, I hid in the nursery. Jeremy found me there and let me help him feed the bears. I was hooked. For a few years, I spent three nights a week with the bears.

"That's how Ella and I became friends. Jeremy ran the sanctuary for seven years. Ella doesn't have much to do with it anymore. She sold it three years ago, but she'll take in cubs for short-term holding. That mama bear and babies will be back in the woods in a few weeks."

The story spun in his head. Ella was married? "What happened to Jeremy?"

"He died."

"How?"

"One of his bears attacked him. He was alone and never stood a chance. When Ella first came home, they named the coffee shop 'The Grizzly Bear.' But when Jeremy died, she and I remodeled the place and renamed it. It was very therapeutic for her. The night after we reopened the shop, the new sanctuary owners called and asked her to take in some cubs. I was shocked when she said yes. She doesn't blame the bear for what happened. Jeremy knew he was taking a risk."

And Theo was just playing with her. They would have a serious talk about Ella later.

They picked up a pizza and took it to Sid's house. Aspen thought his movie education was lacking, and she had every intention of educating him on the merits of blowing things up.

"I'll see your two days of dishes and raise you a week's worth of vacuuming." Rowan laid the homemade chips down and gave his dad an evil glare. Aspen and her mom had already folded, and Sid, having no earthly idea what his was doing, looked at his cards. Two queens, two kings, and an ace. He knew that was enough to win this hand, but he wasn't sure if this was a hand he wanted to win or not.

Theo taught him how to play poker, but Aspen's family played for monthly chores. And Aspen's mom, foreseeing the possibility that everyone would try to lose, instituted a rule that you had to have a least thirty chips in your possession at all times. If you went below thirty, the rest of the family could give you any chips they wanted. And the dreaded bathroom duty chips were the first thrown at the poor sucker who went under thirty chips. Sid knew if bathroom chips were in play, everyone folded. But aside from that, he could never tell if he wanted to win or lose. You only ever wanted to win when the "good" chores were in play.

After Aspen's dad threw in another week of vacuuming, Sid matched with a dusting, since according to Aspen, they were equivalent. Sid won.

Aspen's parents had been a little apprehensive about letting him play with them tonight. Family game night was a sacred tradition every Tuesday. No one missed family game night for anything. Sometimes friends joined in, except on the last Tuesday of the month. That was the night they played for the next month's chores. Sid spent a good thirty minutes convincing Stacey that he wanted to help with the chores.

"But what about your own house. Surely you've got responsibilities there."

"No, we have a housekeeper who does everything. I've never done dishes before or vacuumed. I want to learn how. Seriously." And cross a few more tasks off his *Human Experience* list.

Rowan sat in the chair next to him and popped a few pretzels in his mouth. "Your boyfriend is mental, Aspen."

"I know, but that just means he'll be spending more time around here." She kissed him on the cheek.

"Oh, gag. Mom, I don't want to see this all night."

Aspen's mom grinned. "I think it's sweet. I was beginning to think Aspen wasn't ever going to date. What about you? When are you going to bring a girl home? Honestly, you two are seniors in high school, and this is the first time we've ever had a boyfriend or girlfriend over. By the time Sissy was your age she'd had several."

"I'm not Sissy," Rowan and Aspen said at the same time. Aspen explained that her older sister was the perfect child who could do no wrong. She was only eleven months older than the twins, but had graduated a full year early from school and was now on a full scholarship to a university in Hawaii.

Jason, sat next to her mom. "You have a single housekeeper? I would think in a place like that you'd have to have team."

"We don't keep the whole thing open. We only use about a quarter of the house. There are rooms I've never been in."

Aspen started dividing chips. "It's a cool house though, Sid. Do you mind if I bring my family over to see it sometime? The house is somewhat of a legend in Gardiner."

"Yeah, anyone who wants can see it. I don't care."

"You know, you might want to consider having an open house for the town. The house has been closed up for so many years. People would love to see it," Stacey said.

"I'll mention it to Theo. He'd probably be cool with that."

"Halloween," piped up Aspen.

"What?"

"Everyone thinks that house is haunted. Halloween would be a neat time to open it up. Have a party or something. The whole town would show up."

After they finished the poker game, Aspen came home with him to talk to Theo about the party. He and Ella were watching a movie.

Aspen yelled from the doorway. "You're decent right?"

"Yeah," Ella called back.

Aspen sprawled out on the carpet in front of Ella and Theo. "Epic party. Here. Halloween. What do you think?"

Ella grinned. "That would rock. This house is perfect."

"I was thinking the whole town, kids, adults, everyone," said Aspen.

Sid sat next to Theo. Both girls looked at them.

Sid had no idea what a party like that would entail, so he waited for Theo.

"Okay," he said. "I know a party planner in California. I'll call her up and see if she can help us out."

CHAPTER 29

ON SATURDAY MORNING, Aspen awoke with a start. Roses, she smelled roses. She opened her eyes. Her room had exploded into shades of pink, purple, red, white, and yellow. No surface had been left uncovered. She couldn't see the books on her bookshelf because they were lined with skinny vases, each holding a single red bud. Her computer desk was overflowing with baby pink flowers. Petals of every color covered the floor. And her bed. She tried to pick up a yellow rose covering her body. When she lifted one, the rest followed. It was a blanket of yellow rose heads, all in full bloom.

The note, she knew there had to be a note somewhere. She turned and checked her pillow, nothing. She got up and scanned her desk, nothing but pink. There was a knock on the door.

"Come in," Aspen hollered.

Rowan poked his head in, "Holy smokes, it's like a freakin' florist shop in here. What happened?"

"A note, do you see a note anywhere?"

"Oh yeah, check the bathroom."

Aspen pushed him out of the way and ran for the bathroom. Written on her mirror were three words. "Go see Ella."

She took the fastest shower in human history and flew to the PD. It was packed. Where the nights belonged to the teenagers, Saturday mornings belonged to the old folks. Ella was serving Mrs. Walker. Aspen tapped her foot.

As soon as Mrs. Walker left, Aspen spoke. "You have something for me."

"You're a little impatient. First, tell me about your room. Sid didn't tell me what he did. He just said to ask you."

Aspen explained all about the flowers, and Ella handed her the largest mocha they had.

"You're not allowed to leave until it's gone."

Aspen scowled and sat down. She scalded her tongue as she slurped down the mocha. Ella didn't have to make it so hot.

She people watched while she drank. Matt's parents came in, and her stomach clenched. She hadn't seen them since the funeral. They waved to her, and she smiled, but they moved away from her. She was grateful she didn't have to talk to them.

Her cup was now almost empty. Inside was a message. "Go home. Find your dad."

She tossed the cup, and Ella yelled from behind the counter as she raced for the door. "Details, Aspen, I want details tomorrow."

Aspen cringed. Her definition of details and Ella's were completely different. Aspen repeatedly told her she didn't need all the gory facts, but Ella still told her things like the color of her thong she wore to Theo's house, and well, Aspen didn't like thinking about the rest of the details.

She went sixty the whole way home despite the fact the speed limit was forty. Her dad met her in the garage and handed her a pack through the jeep window.

"What's this?"

"Everything you'll need for an overnight hike."

Aspen's stomach did flip-flops, and she wasn't sure if it was because of excitement or nerves.

"Any idea where I'm supposed to go?"

"Oh, yeah, you are supposed to go to the Tower-Roosevelt Visitor Center. Be safe, Aspen. I trust you. Don't give me a reason not to."

"Of course, Dad."

He kissed her on the top of her head and backed away.

Aspen drove slowly through the park. The weather was getting colder, things were changing. She felt the change in herself as well. She'd withdrawn from her friends. Nearly two months had passed since she first saw Obsidian up on the hill, and both he and Sid had now taken over her life. It was strange how when she grew closer to one, she grew closer to the other.

Obsidian was her best friend. Sid was like an extension of herself. She'd never felt this way about anyone before. It was so easy to be with him. Nothing was forced, everything flowed. Except of course, when he reminded her of Marc. Then she freaked, and he got hurt. If only Sid didn't look so hauntingly like him.

The visitor center was nearly empty. The ranger recognized her and handed her a box and an envelope. Aspen opened the envelope first.

"Go shoot some ducks on your thumb." So far none of Sid's messages had been cryptic, so this one confused her. She took the box out to her car and opened it. A new camera. An expensive new camera. "Shoot." That had to mean taking a picture. "Thumb." Hmm, ah, Duck Lake at West Thumb. She got it.

The road to the West Thumb was long, and Aspen was getting impatient. The scavenger hunt was fun, but she was ready to be with Sid. She wasn't sure exactly what she was looking for at Duck Lake, but she was determined to find it quickly.

A bench sat on the edge of the lake. On top was a small backpack. Aspen picked it up. Sure enough the zipper had a small padlock on it. Attached to one of the straps was a large tag. "You know where to go. See you soon."

Aspen remembered the conversation they had right before she kissed him the first time. Heart Lake.

Sid was leaning against his car, waiting. Aspen threw her arms around his neck and kissed him.

"Well, I guess that was the reaction I was looking for," he said.

"I love you," Aspen blurted without thinking.

He flinched.

Uh-oh. Aspen tried to think of a way to take back those words. She meant them, but he obviously wasn't ready to hear them. What if this was all a game to him? What if he was like Marc?

"Sorry, I meant that I love what you did for me. The flowers, the camera. I love it all."

"Aspen…"

"Really, I didn't mean it."

He grinned. "Yes, you did. Stop trying to deny it. I love you too. Come on, let's go."

Sid loved and hated those three words. He knew she had sealed herself to him, but something about the words made it final. She loved him. He would never be able to love another. When she died, Sid would ache for his remaining years. Taking a queen would be pointless. He was a failure as king.

The path was narrow, and she walked a couple of feet in front of him. Her two braids swung from side to side as she navigated the terrain. She stopped, turned, and looked at him.

"Did you have a girlfriend before you moved here?"

Sid wondered what brought that on. "Yeah."

Her face was expressionless. "Tell me about her."

She turned around and kept walking.

"You really want me to?"

"No, but I need to know."

"Skye and I were together for a long time. Everyone assumed we'd end up together forever. It was so comfortable that I just let it continue until fate stepped in and ended it."

"I asked you to tell me about her. Not your relationship."

Sid hesitated, not sure how much or exactly what to tell her. "Skye was beautiful. I think that is what first attracted me to her. That and she was incredibly sweet. She didn't have a mean bone in her body. She was a great companion and friend, but she lacked the qualities I was looking for in a girlfriend."

Aspen was quiet for a long time.

"Did I make you angry?" he asked.

"No," she replied. "I'm just wondering exactly what you're looking for."

Sid laughed. "Actually, I didn't know what I wanted until I found you. You're funny, smart, and passionate. You see the world as a place to be conquered, not just lived in. You attack every task, everything in life, with such zeal. I can hardly keep up with you. Do you realize that I practically fell in love with you before we even met?"

She laughed. "What are you talking about?"

"You know that picture in the PD that you took? The one of the violet dragon?"

"Yeah"

"Ella showed that to me when she gave me a tour of the place. I knew that any girl brave enough to take a picture of a dragon was worth getting to know. I as much as told Ella that too."

"And what did she say?"

"She told me you were going to hate me."

Aspen laughed hard, shattering the silence of the forest.

"I never want this to end," she said.

"Why would it have to?" Sid asked. He knew human relationships were different from dragons'. However, he didn't quite understand how she could talk about an end to a relationship that just began.

"We're in high school. Next year you'll be going off to college. Long distance relationships never last." She sighed.

"That's easy to fix. I'll go wherever you decide to go. Where is that by the way? I should probably start making plans." Sid still didn't understand why there might be a problem.

"You can't just say you'll go wherever I go. What if you decide later that you don't want to be with me? Then you'll be stuck going to a school you don't want to go to with a girl you don't want to be with. Besides, I'm not going to college. I'm going to get a camera crew and search for more dragons."

"Why would I not want to be with you? I just told you I loved you. I've never told anyone that before. Love doesn't just change its mind." Sid fumed. How could a girl he loved so much make him so angry?

"Why don't you trust me?" Sid asked.

She turned and looked at him again, her face full of sadness. Sid felt the fear that so often plagued her when they first met. She didn't speak again. She set up the tent while he built the fire. They ate in silence, Sid unsure of how to start the conversation after she basically admitted she didn't trust him.

It was dark by the time they finished. They went into the tent and both burrowed into their sleeping bags. Aspen scooted over so she was close to him. He put his hand on her cheek, and she smiled at him. After a few more minutes of silence, she spoke.

"Three years ago my parents took me to Yosemite for the summer. I was young and stupid." She hesitated. "I wanted, well, I wanted a lot of things that summer. Mostly though, I wanted to be noticed by boys—to be loved and kissed." Her voice cracked, and he pulled her close to him. "This sounds so pathetic. Sid, promise me that no matter what I tell you tonight, you won't think less of me."

"I promise."

"I fell in with a group of girls who taught me how to get noticed. I ran around in string bikinis, short shorts, and a lot of makeup. I must've looked so desperate. However, I got the attention I was looking for. One night, at a party at the lodge, I met Marc Ford.

"Marc looked just like you. He had brown eyes instead of blue, and his nose was a little bigger, but aside from that, you could've been his twin. When you showed up at the PD the night of the back-to-school party, I thought for sure he had come back to torture me."

Her guilt was overwhelming. Almost powerful enough to overcome his growing anger with Marc.

She continued. "We flirted shamelessly, and I had my first kiss. I was elated. We spent every waking minute together. After a few days, he started pushing me to go further than I was comfortable with. And then he uttered those three magic words, 'I love you.'

"The next night we went for a drive. He talked me into going all the way. He called it 'making love.' At that time, I thought I really did love him. I was convinced I would spend the rest of my life with him." She paused and shuddered. "I showed up to a party at the lodge the next day, and he was making out with a new blonde hottie. I was crushed. I had fully given myself to him, and he went off and found someone else to take."

Aspen's body shook with sobs, and Sid held her close. "I'm so sorry."

She pulled away and faced him. "I'm not done."

CHAPTER 30

Three Years Ago

THE CLOUD COVERING the sun made perfect lighting for Aspen's pictures. The giant trees rose all around her. It was peaceful.

Away from Marc and his horrid deception. Away from her family and their curious stares. Away from Brittany and Cat and the pity. Trees didn't care what she'd done or the shame she had.

Aspen climbed out of the grove of trees into a circular meadow surrounded by the giant sequoias. A doe grazed in the middle of the field. Aspen crouched and started snapping, but before she got even a few pictures, the doe saw her and took off. Aspen hiked to the middle of the field and reveled in the silence. She scanned the sky, always on the lookout for her dragons.

A large purple mass flew in her direction, and she focused and zoomed. The dragon was lavender and had leaf-green wings. She flew almost directly over Aspen. As Aspen took the picture, arms snaked around her, and a voice whispered in her ear.

"You look so sexy when you're excited."

Aspen tried to pull away, but he held her close.

"Let me go."

She fought Marc's arms. She didn't want to drop her camera, but she was starting to panic. He squeezed her tighter.

"Don't think I'll do that." His voice dropped to a whisper. "I want you, Aspen. I want you bad. I've been searching all over for you, but you've been avoiding me."

He held her with one arm and used the other to rip the camera from her hands. He tossed it a few yards away. His free hand wove its way into her hair and pulled. Her eyes watered.

"If you just want sex, why don't you go find blondie?"

"Oh where's the fun in that? I knew you'd fight me. This is much more exciting."

His other arm released her, but he held tight to her hair. Aspen risked her scalp and tried to run. It didn't rip from her head like she wanted it to. He pulled back, and Aspen's body slammed into the ground. Marc climbed on top of her, straddling her body.

Aspen squirmed as he traced a finger down her face. "Poor, Aspen, so scared, so angry, and so ashamed." He leaned down and whispered in her ear. "And so damn sexy."

She pushed his face away and punched him. She saw a blur of movement, and her face exploded with pain. Blood trickled down her temple.

"You won't look very pretty when I'm done."

Aspen screamed. She knew it was pointless. She picked that trail this morning because she knew it was deserted. Marc swung his fist, and she moved to block it. His hand slammed into the hard ground, and he howled with rage.

She rolled over, and his boot slammed into her kidneys. She lay on the ground, breathing hard. She saw no way out, but she wouldn't let him rape her. She'd fight him to the death. She pushed off from the ground again, heard a loud crack, and registered the blinding pain on the back of her head. All went black.

Her eyes barely opened. They were swollen shut. She tasted dirt. She lifted her head and found that awful face of Marc. His hand was resting on her stomach.

"I told you you'd cooperate. You were wonderful by the way, but I wish you could've been awake. Let this be a lesson to you not to fight so hard next time."

He stood, and she realized she was naked. He held all her clothes in his hands.

"I think I'll take these with me. Enjoy your humiliation." He turned and sauntered off into the surrounding forest.

Aspen's head was pounding. She struggled to stand, but everything hurt. She found her camera and went in search of her bag. She was grateful she left it in the forest. She never went hiking anywhere without a change of clothes. As she dressed, she tried to think of possible stories. The police wouldn't help. Due to her penchant for danger, she'd had a few run-ins with cops over the years, and she knew involving them would be useless. A bear attack made the most sense. She told no one what really happened.

CHAPTER 31

THAT IS WHY I do not trust you, Sid. You look so much like him. I have to remind myself every day that you are not him." Marc Ford. Otherwise known as Marcellus. Sid's own cousin. How could he do something like this? Sid wondered how many other girls he'd violated. His human years were about to be cut short, and he would die a very painful death.

Aspen was still shuddering in his arms when Sid forced her chin up. "Aspen, I love you. What he did to you is not your fault. Someday I will find Marc Ford and kill him."

She smiled. "That won't fix anything. I don't want to talk about this anymore. Can we let it go?"

She fell asleep in his arms. He lay awake for a long time thinking about the fact that every time he spoke to her, it was a lie. He was not who he said he was, and neither was Obsidian. They were the same and by keeping that from her, he was deceiving her. Tomorrow he would tell her everything.

CHAPTER 32

LILA FALLS WASN'T crazy about camping. Quite frankly, she didn't have time for it. She should be home studying or working on her college applications. But Dan kept her sane, so that meant, occasionally, she had to do dumb things like camping.

It was cold when she got up the next morning to start the fire. Usually Dan did that, but she wanted to surprise him and prove she was capable.

She stacked the wood like she'd seen him do a thousand times and stuck a fire starter in the middle. Then she lit the tip with a lighter. To her surprise it worked the first time. She rocked back on her heels, thoroughly pleased.

She heard the zipper on the tent open. Dan poked his head out.

"Look what I did," Lila said.

He grinned. "I see that. Good job. We'll make an outdoorsy girl out of you yet."

Lila grimaced. That was not what she wanted. Maybe starting the fire had been a stupid idea.

"I'm going to get dressed. I'll be out in a second." Dan disappeared into the tent. Lila stood and stretched. The sound of flapping wings came from above her. They didn't sound right though. They were louder than a bird's wings should be. More like a slapping sound. She looked up.

It took her a second but she screamed as a huge golden dragon flew toward her. The dragon opened its mouth, and Lila was no more.

The dragon flew away, confident that this time, he hadn't left behind any evidence of his meal. What he didn't see, though, was her boyfriend sticking his head out the tent just before the dragon's jaws scooped up the girl.

CHAPTER 33

SID WOKE ALONE the next morning. He exited the tent and found Aspen next to the fire fiddling with the backpack. Her mood had shifted. She was excited, happy. She pointed to the lock.

"You have the key, right?"

"Of course."

"I think I've waited long enough."

"Okay, but you know how you made me promise not to think less of you yesterday?"

Her expression fell. "Yeah."

"Can you do the same for me? You're not the only one with a secret. Promise me you'll still love me, no matter what that bag holds."

"Sure, can I have the key now?"

Sid held his hand out. Aspen reached for the key and a scream pierced the silence. Sid dropped the key.

They looked up as racing footsteps approached. Dan burst through the trees with an ashen face.

Aspen hurried over to him. "Are you okay?"

He panted and shook his head. Tears flowed down his cheeks.

She put her hand on his shoulder. "Dan, you gotta talk to us. What happened?"

"A dragon," he said.

Aspen looked at Sid, her face beaming. "What about a dragon?"

"A giant gold dragon. He got Lila. She's…she's gone."

Her expression changed from excitement to horror.

Sid's mind raced through the possibilities. Marcellus. It had to be Marcellus. No other dragon would be that vicious. Sid wouldn't have suspected him, except that he destroyed Aspen. He was the only dragon capable of such brutality. The humans would believe that all the dragons were monsters. It would be too late to warn the humans now. They would not trust the dragons.

Aspen gave Dan some water.

Sid pulled her aside. "Aspen, you okay?"

"No. I didn't think dragons were capable of this."

"Neither did I." Of course Sid knew that it was a dragon, but he couldn't let on that he knew before today, or she'd get suspicious. If he were being honest with himself though, he was still having trouble believing it.

"They will never be looked at the same way again. As soon as Dan's story shows up on the news, people will be crying for blood. They will hunt them."

"I don't think it will be that bad."

"Yeah, it will be that bad. And I don't want to go to another funeral. Before this year, nobody I knew had ever died. Now I'll be attending the funeral of yet another one of my friends."

"Come on, let's pack up and get out of here. We need to tell the park rangers what happened."

They hastily packed up and headed down the mountain. They left Dan at the visitor center, and Sid promised the rangers he'd take Aspen to her parents. Then he raced home to talk to Theo. Marcellus needed to be stopped. Now.

CHAPTER 34

SID SPRAYED GRAVEL as he flew up the driveway. In his blind fury, he saw nothing as he ran to the door. But as he reached the porch, he tripped and caught himself on the wall next to the door. At his feet lay Talbot. Dead. His heart clenched. First Matt, then Lila, now Talbot. He didn't know how much more death he could take.

He gathered the bird in his arms, looking for injuries. There were no obvious ones. Someone must've broken his neck. He had to have seen something that Marcellus wanted to keep quiet. It was a shame he had to die when Sid already knew the truth.

Theo wasn't high enough up on the political chain to be much help. Sid changed and flew off to see Pearl.

He scared a couple of hikers as he flew over the Red Mountains and found a sleeping Pearl in a cave just south of Heart Lake.

Pearl, he said, *I need to you wake up.*

She opened one eye. *What are you doing here? I thought we discussed you not leaving your human form.*

I know, but something came up. Something the council should know.

Sid told her about Lila and the things Aspen had told him, deliberately leaving out her name. He could feel Pearl's emotions change from irritation to anger. Pearl was always so levelheaded, and her fury surprised Sid. She thought for a few minutes.

How Marcellus could do something like this is beyond me. He was always cocky, but I never imagined he would be this brutal. Let's stop and think for a minute. We know what he did to this girl, but are we sure he's the one eating the humans?

Who else would do such a thing?

There are hundreds of gold dragons. It could be any one of them.

None of them raped an innocent girl.

True. If I take this to the council, you know what will happen to him.

Yes, Sid replied. *And I would like to deliver the punishment.*

She looked at him and cocked her head to the side. *Sid, I lived with the humans for ten years, and most girls would only share that story with someone for one of two reasons. Either they were looking for attention or they completely loved and trusted the person they were sharing it with.*

Sid shifted uneasily and squatted down so she couldn't see his mark. *Aspen trusts me.*

Aspen?

Yes.

The one you told me you could handle? The one you sealed yourself to.

Yes.

Pearl bristled. *Sid, you do understand the consequences if she seals herself to you, right?*

Yes, I do. And I am being careful, but I won't stay away from her.

You've put me in a very difficult position. As a member of the council, it is my duty to ensure that you're doing as instructed. I must report all that you have told me. The consequences will not be pleasant.

I don't care what you tell them as long as you make sure Marcellus is taken care of.

Of course, she sighed. *You should leave though.*

What are you going to do about the humans being aware it's one of us?

We will send ambassadors, and no, you can't be one of them. That part will be fine. We should be able to get to Dan before he tells anyone else. We'll bring a canyon dragon with us. He can muddle with the boy's memory so he won't remember a dragon actually being involved. Locating Marcellus could be difficult though.

Remember, I get to kill him.

Only if you are still alive.

What's that supposed to mean?

You really think the council is going to ignore your rendezvous with Aspen?

They have bigger problems with Marcellus.

You are living in a dream world. The council can deal with more than one issue. Now, go.

CHAPTER 35

A LL BACKCOUNTRY HIKING was banned in Yellowstone. Aspen's parents forbade her from outdoor activity all together.

The funeral was Tuesday. Aspen and Sid spent most of the day with friends from school. That evening they drove to Sid's house.

"Why didn't Dan say anything about the dragon? He told us it was a gold dragon, but now he acts like he has no idea what happened. That Lila just disappeared."

Sid kept his eyes on the road. "I don't know."

"That's BS. You do so know. You didn't seem surprised when nothing was in the papers about the dragon, or today when Tori asked Dan what happened. His story had changed. You know."

It was time to fix this. If Dan hadn't interrupted their breakfast, Aspen would know already.

"Okay. So there is something. Aspen, I want to tell you, I really do. But right now the dragons have a huge mess on their hands, and I won't make things worse by dragging you into it. As soon as this dragon is caught and disposed of, I'll tell you everything."

"No. This has gone on long enough. Both you and Obsidian have some explaining to do. In fact, I think the next time I visit him, you need to come with me. Let's clear the air once and for all. I'm already in the middle of the dragon mess."

Sid sighed. She was right. He wanted her to know the truth anyway. He just hoped she would still talk to him after he told her.

"I need to go get something. After that we'll drive out into the park and get this over with."

"Really?" Aspen grinned at him, and her feelings abruptly shifted to sheer excitement. This had been a mystery she'd been dying to solve.

Sid wanted to grab the backpack he'd given Aspen on the hike. It had things in there that would make it easier to explain. They walked through the kitchen; seated at the kitchen table were Theo, Ella, and a petite blonde woman wearing a black dress and red heels. She straightened her pointed glasses and held out her hand.

"You must be Sid." Her grip was firm, confident. "And, Aspen, I'm so sorry for your loss." She gave Aspen a hug. Aspen's eyes bugged, but the woman didn't seem to notice. "I'm Vicki. Theo's party planner. I've missed him since he left. He threw the best parties in LA since he had an unlimited budget. But that is beside the point. We have a Halloween party to plan, and this house is absolutely perfect. Come, sit."

Sid moved toward the table, but Aspen held him back. "I'm not so sure a party would be a good idea anymore. The whole community is grieving, and they will be for some time."

Ella spoke up. "Actually, Aspen, the party is a month away. It'll be good for the community to look forward to something. I don't think it will be a problem."

Aspen crossed her arms. "Fine. But we have something to do. You three can do this without us."

"Come on, this will take all of thirty minutes. Sit," Theo said.

Aspen reluctantly climbed on one of the stools and gave Sid a glare. He grimaced and mouthed, "Sorry."

Vicki laid out vintage pictures. A man with nails puncturing his face, a bearded woman, a man with enormous muscles, and a two-headed snake. "I thought a good theme would be a freak show. We'll bring in sword and fire swallowers, pinheads, strange and exotic animals. The whole nine yards."

Ella studied the pictures. "What about food?"

"Carnival and fair food, of course. Corn dogs, french fries, elephant ears. And we'll have carnival games set up throughout. What do you think?"

Sid shrugged. Parties would be new for him, so he didn't know if this was normal or not. Ella took over. "This is fine."

Theo nodded, and Aspen took the pictures from Ella.

"Fantastic," Vicki exclaimed. "I'll get on it right away. We'll need to set up a few days before. I only need a couple more things from you all before I leave. Costumes. This is Halloween, so everyone will need to be dressed up. For Theo and Sid, I was thinking typical freak show hosts. Tux, top hat, and bushy mustache. But I haven't come up with anything for the girls yet."

"I want to be the bearded lady," Ella said.

"That's easy. What about you, Aspen, what do you want to be?"

She laid a picture in front of Vicki. "This is who I want to be."

The picture was a faded black and yellow postcard. In the center was a busty woman wearing what looked like a bikini top and a flowing skirt. Her feet were bare. In her hands she held an enormous snake, which wrapped itself around her body.

Vicki gasped. "Oh perfect, you can be Serpentina."

CHAPTER 36

T HE THIRTY-MINUTE meeting turned into two hours, and by the time Vicki left, it was too late to do anything. Plus, Aspen's parents were twitchy about her being out after curfew, which meant she had to be home at nine on the dot.

Just as Aspen was about to get out of the car, Sid handed her the backpack.

"Bring this with you tomorrow when you go see Obsidian. I'll meet you there."

"How do you know where 'there' is?"

"You're too nosy for your own good. Tomorrow everything will be clear, I promise."

He kissed her, and she forgot all about why she was supposed to be mad at him. Damn him for distracting her like that.

The next morning Aspen woke up way too early. She wasn't meeting Obsidian until ten and racked her brain trying to find the connection between him and Sid. She felt as if she was on the brink of understanding something, but it eluded her. She pulled out her computer and flipped through the pictures she'd taken of the dragons. How did Sid fit in? She found the pictures of the silver dragon. They were the best pictures she had ever taken of a dragon. She was gorgeous. Sid had been with her that day. The dragon had stared at him when she landed in the courtyard. Almost as if she had been having a conversation with him.

Of course she had. Why? It wasn't fair that Sid got to be part of their world and she couldn't.

Who was Sid? A messenger of sorts for the dragons? She'd never seen Obsidian and Sid together. But that could be because they knew they'd have a crapload of questions to answer for her. Or was it possible….

Could Sid be a dragon? Could they shapeshift? She supposed stranger things were possible. She knew dragons had magic.

Aspen shook her head. No, that was stupid. More often than not though, Aspen thought of Sid and Obsidian interchangeably.

She got up and moved to window, tripping over something. It was the backpack. The same one from when they went camping. The zipper was still locked. She ran to the garage and got the wire cutters. The lock came off easily.

The backpack held an old tattered book. There was no title page, just a list—a very long list. She paused to read a few of the lines. There was a checkmark next to "Take a math class," but not next to "Get a high school diploma." What was this? She flipped farther and saw "Kiss a girl" checked.

She closed the book, reached into the backpack, and pulled out a framed picture of the silver dragon. There was a Post-it note with the words "My sister" scrawled across it in Sid's handwriting.

Aspen's heart raced. She dropped the picture. How was this possible?

She picked up the book and flipped through the pages again. It must be a to do list of sorts. Was she just some project from the book? Something Sid or Obsidian could mark off so that he could say he did it?

Everything made sense, and it pissed her off. Obsidian or Sid or whatever his name was lied to her. Repeatedly. Oh, he was so in for it.

The clock seemed to move more slowly that morning. The more time that passed, the angrier she got. She supposed she could just call Sid and ask him to come over, but she wanted to see him as Obsidian, and her backyard was too small for that.

At a quarter to nine, she laced up her boots, put on her coat and gloves, grabbed the backpack, and headed out on the trail that led away from her house.

Obsidian was already in the clearing when she arrived. Her anger nearly dissipated. Her heart constricted. She loved both of them, and they were the same. She should be happy, but he'd lied to her.

"I know what you can do. I want to see your human form."

How do you know?

She held up the backpack and the broken lock.

"I'm waiting," she finally said.

Watching him change was one of the strangest things Aspen had ever seen. His body shrank. Claws became fingers, and a snout became a nose. It took less than thirty seconds.

She sank to the ground. In spite of the evidence she had, she still wasn't quite expecting it. Sid held a hand out to her. She swatted it away and stood up on her own.

"Why'd you lie to me?"

"I tried to tell you, but I never quite got it out. I'm so sorry."

She'd forgotten what kind of effect he had on her. He sounded so sincere. She wanted to reach out and touch his face, and she had an overwhelming desire to kiss him. Focus, she reminded herself.

"You didn't tell me though. You seemed so shocked that I couldn't trust you, yet our whole relationship is a lie. I can't even seem to reconcile that you and Obsidian are the same."

He took her hands in his, his eyes seeking hers. "I'm so sorry. Please forgive me."

Aspen closed her eyes, gathering her anger, and opened them again. She ripped her hands from his. "What about the book? Was I just a task to mark off on your stupid list? You are just like Marc. I never should've trusted you."

Sid glared at her. "I'm nothing like Marc. Don't you dare make that comparison."

"I was a joke to you. A mission so you could finish whatever it is you're supposed to do here."

Sid pinched the bridge of his nose. "It's true I used parts of our relationship to mark off things in that stupid book, but believe me, I'm in much more trouble than you can imagine. I liked you, and I used the book as an excuse to get close to you, but both Theo and Pearl were against it from the very beginning. They were right. I shouldn't have fallen in love with you, and I certainly didn't expect you to reciprocate. But it happened. I love you. You have to believe that."

Aspen crossed her arms. "And why the hell should I believe you?"

Sid leaned down and peeled away his sock, revealing the tattoo with her name.

"Because this proves it. This ties me to you forever. I will never love another."

"Is that true?"

"Of course it's true. When you die, I will live out my remaining years alone."

She crossed her arms. "How do I know you aren't lying to me again?"

He gripped at his hair. "I don't know how else to tell you this, Aspen. I'm madly in love with you. No stupid book will change that."

Aspen's heart caught in her throat.

"You still lied to me."

His face fell. "I know. But Aspen, I didn't know how you would react."

Aspen didn't want to be angry with him.

"No more lies."

"No more lies. Now, it's freezing out here. Let's go to your house. I imagine you have a lot of questions."

"That is the understatement of the year."

He took her hand, and she didn't bother pulling away. He was forgiven, and he knew it.

Aspen didn't say much as they walked, her mind reeling with this new information. The house was quiet when they got home. Rowan was probably still in his room playing video games.

They sat on the couch, and Aspen asked the question that had been bothering her since she realized Sid and Obsidian were one in the same.

"What do we do now?"

"What do you mean?"

"You're a dragon, and I'm…well…I'm not."

Sid laughed and scooted closer to her. "That hasn't been a problem so far, has it?"

She shook her head. "But what about the future and the other dragons? Surely this isn't allowed."

"You're right. It's not. But we don't need to worry about that now. As long as they don't find out, we're fine."

"And when they do?"

"We'll deal with it. Aspen, I want you to be a part of my life."

She grinned and laughed. Sid pulled away.

"What's so funny?"

She shook her head and continued giggling.

"I'm sorry," she said when she finally stopped. She moved closer to Sid and took both his hands in hers.

"My boyfriend's a dragon. It's like a complete dream come true for me. But anyone else in the world would be horrified."

Sid smiled.

"It's a good thing I fell in love with you then, instead of someone else."

She nodded. "Definitely a good thing."

CHAPTER 37

E LLA HAD BEEN right about the community looking forward to the party. For two weeks prior, Sid's phone rang off the hook—half the time it was people from town and the other half was Vicki. Apparently, this party would reach epic proportions. It would be Vicki's biggest yet—and most expensive. People from all over the county would be coming because Sid's house was about to be opened up for the first time in a hundred years. People wanted to see the inside. Not that it would look like it normally does.

The weather was too cold to hold anything outside so his entire house would be transformed into a carnival. The basement would hold all the rides. The main level would be food and entertainers, and the upper level would have various freak shows and games. Costumes were mandatory.

Three days before the party, Sid hid out in his room to avoid Vicki, who was attempting to ask his opinion on everything from the exact placement of the candied apples to which room would best for the sword swallower. He kept telling her he didn't care; she was the expert.

Someone knocked on the door.

"I already told you, Vicki. Use your best judgment." But when the door opened, it was Pearl.

She sat at his computer desk, her face a mask of no emotion. "What are they doing to your house?"

"We're having a party on Halloween. You should come, bring Raja with you. But you have to wear costumes."

"Will Aspen be at the party?"

"Of course."

"It's time to fix the Aspen problem."

"Nope, it's not. What about Marcellus? Have you caught him yet?"

"We're still looking. He's been evasive. But every dragon guard is out searching for him. Including most of the council."

"Sid, can you hear me?" asked Aspen from the other side of the phone.

"Just barely, where are you? I thought you'd be here by now." The party started thirty minutes ago, and his date was still missing.

"I know. My parents just got home, and I promised I'd wait for them. They're getting dressed. We'll be there in fifteen."

"Okay, hurry up though. Vicki's having a fit because her Serpentina isn't here yet."

"Yep, love you. I'll see you soon."

Vicki had certainly done her best making over the house. They moved all the furniture into two large trucks that were now parked in the Purple Dragon's lot.

Theo and Ella acted the perfect hosts in the entryway. Theo was a bit distracted because his bearded lady was running around in a tiny bikini, having the time of her life.

"Where's Aspen?" Ella asked when Sid approached.

"On her way. Her parents were running late."

She grinned, greeted another family, and handed them a map. "Food is to your right and straight through to the grand room. Rooms that are off limits are marked with a staff only sign. Otherwise everything else is open. If you go up to the second floor, the rooms all have games and freak shows.

"Make sure you go down to the end of the east wing and see the fortuneteller." She looked up at the parents. "Both towers are open, but the farther up you go, the scarier the shows get. And it's PG-13, so I wouldn't take your little ones up there."

She got down on her knees and looked very seriously at the miniature witch and wizard in front of her. "The midgets all have candy, and the louder you yell 'trick or treat' the more candy they'll give you."

Vicki approached from his right. "I need to hire her to host all my parties."

"Yeah," Sid said as Ella went to greet a family of fairies. "But I don't think your dwarfs will appreciate her telling the kids to yell loud."

"Oh well. They're actors used to doing strange things. The one upstairs with the sword swallower yells back. Most of the kids run away before he can give them any candy. Shame because he's got full size candy bars. Those kids brave enough to wait it out are rewarded. Now where's my snake lady?" She put her hands on her hips and waited for a response. The effect was quite humorous as she was a half man, half woman. The bearded side of her face did not match the lipstick.

"On her way. I'm a little hungry. What do you recommend?"

That got a smile out of her. She had bragged the last two weeks about the food. She found it hard to believe Sid had never been to a fair. "The corn dogs are to die for. Or you could try the funnel cakes. Everything is good. Go pick."

Sid dodged midgets and screaming kids and made his way into the great room, nearly running into a man on stilts. The bright green and blue cotton candy caught his eye, so he tried that first. The fibers stuck to his fingers and tasted sickly sweet. Not his kind of food. Ella would probably eat it, though. Sid snatched a corn dog from a man in torn clothes with a permanent snarl and turned to go to the entryway when he caught sight of Aspen.

Her back was to his, but his heart stopped anyway. Above her bare feet, her marking stood out. On her left ankle she had an airbrushed tattoo, but it was bright green and contained her name instead of his. Her own tribute to Obsidian.

She wore sheer green gypsy pants that hung low on her hips. Her nearly bare back had another airbrushed tattoo, a black dragon with a golden belly. Her black-dyed hair curled and hung down to her shoulder blades.

Sid snuck up on her from behind and slid his hand across her bare stomach and pulled her toward him.

"How am I supposed to host a party when you look this hot? All I want to do is take you to my room," Sid whispered in her ear. She laughed, and he found himself face-to-face with beady black eyes and a forked tongue. The snake stared at him for a half second before it opened his mouth and hissed. Sid let go of Aspen and turned her around.

She looked even better, except for the snake weaving itself around her body, into her hair, and down her back. They were a few species dragons couldn't communicate with. Snakes were one of them.

"I don't think your snake likes me much."

"Yeah, probably not."

"Course, I don't like him much either. I'm a little jealous that he gets to crawl all over you. I was under the impression I was the only one who got to do that."

She blushed and wove her fingers into his. "Come on, I want to see the rest of the party."

He held her at arm's length and looked her up and down again, wondering how the hell he'd manage to stare at her all night and refrain from doing things not fit for the public eye. His eyes trailed down to her ankles, and his heart froze. He hadn't thought about the implications.

"You need to cover your tattoos."

"Why?"

"My sister is coming tonight, and she can't see those."

Aspen's eyes bugged. "Your sister is coming? You mean I get to meet another dragon?"

"Yeah, but, for obvious reasons, she can't know that you know about us."

He stopped one of the actors who had leather cuffs around his wrists. "Can I have those?"

"Your party. Sure." The man took off the cuffs and handed them to him.

Aspen fastened the cuffs to her ankles, and Sid sighed. Pearl would have a fit if she saw the markings.

"You hungry?" Sid asked, hoping for another corn dog.

Aspen shook her head and dragged him up the stairs. They played a few games and he won her a stuffed dragon by hitting a balloon with a sharp dart. At the end of the east wing they visited the fortuneteller. She gave them their fortunes together. Told them they'd get married, have ten kids, and live until they were a hundred. Sid grimaced because he already passed his five hundredth birthday and would be lucky to see another one.

CHAPTER 38

SPEN THOUGHT THE night couldn't have been more perfect. Sid looked adorable with his bushy mustache and top hat. Except it tickled her cheek when he kissed her. The snake Vicki's people loaned her was docile, except he didn't like Sid. Although the feeling was mutual. After a visit to the fortuneteller, they were about to make their way up the towers to see the truly freaky and weird when Sid stiffened next to her.

"Are you okay?" she asked.

He nodded, but his eyes were on a tall girl with dark red hair. She wore a golden dress with long sleeves and showed generous cleavage. Her arm was looped through the arm of a man who had the same dark skin and black hair as Sid, but his hair was cut short.

"Aspen," she said, untangling herself from the man and taking Aspen's hands in hers. "It's fabulous to finally meet you. Sid has told me so much about you. You are every bit as gorgeous as he said. And what a clever costume." Aspen couldn't tell if she was being genuine or if she was mocking her in some way. Sid had a frown on his face. Or at least Aspen thought he did. It was hard to tell from the mustache. "Sid, aren't you going to introduce us?"

He put his arm around Aspen's waist. Her snake, who had been hiding in her hair, peeked his head out and hissed at Sid again. Sid gripped her ribs a little harder, but he didn't move from her side.

"Aspen, this is my sister Pearl and her fiancé Raja."

Raja grimaced when Sid said fiancé.

"Wow, Sid didn't tell me there was going to be a wedding in the family. When's the big day?" Aspen asked.

Pearl looped her arm through Raja's again and put on a sugary smile. "We haven't set a date yet." She looked at Sid. "Raja's dying to see Theo again. Why don't you help find him, and I'll stay and get to know Aspen a little better?"

Sid pulled Aspen back as a couple of kids ran down the hall. "Aspen and I were just about to go up the tower. Why don't you join us, and then we'll all go and find Theo." He didn't wait for Pearl's response.

Before Aspen knew what was happening, Sid had her halfway up the stairs. The first room they stopped at had purple fabric draped on the walls. Eerie green lamps hung from the ceiling and a vintage desk with an ancient sewing machine sat in the corner. A woman with a pixie face and bobbed hair sat beneath the chandelier. She would've been cute but for the eight legs curling under her skirt. She flexed three of the legs and wrapped one around her neck. Aspen grimaced, and Pearl spoke.

"Sid, this is disgusting. Why would you have a party with this filth?"

"If you don't like it, go back downstairs and wait. We'll be done soon."

"I'm not leaving you alone with that girl anymore."

Pearl had been so friendly so far that her words surprised Aspen. She looked at Sid. He and Pearl were staring at each other. Probably having a conversation in their heads that she wasn't invited to. Not fair. Aspen put herself in between Sid and Pearl. "Look, you have something you want to say to me. Why don't you just say it?"

Pearl pursed her lips and glared. Raja looked at Sid and raised his eyebrows.

Sid spoke up. "Pearl, it's obvious I shouldn't have invited you. I'm sorry you have a problem with Aspen, but I think it's time for you to leave."

Wuss. He didn't want Aspen to listen to what Pearl had to say. "No, Sid, I think we need to hear her out. She's your sister. I don't want to create a rift. Why won't she let you be alone with me anymore?"

"He's not allowed to be with you. You threaten everything."

"Look, I know a lot more than you think I do. We'll figure it out."

Pearl sneered. "There is where you are wrong, sweetheart. I don't know what Sid told you, but you don't know anything, or you would stay away from him. He's been promised to another. You threaten that. Stay out of his life."

Aspen felt as if someone had slapped her. Not two weeks ago, Sid practically swore he'd spend the rest of his life with her. What had Pearl meant when she said he was promised to someone else?

Pearl turned and swept down the stairs with Raja following.

"Sid, what the hell was that all about? Is there some dragon waiting for you?"

Sid pressed his lips against hers. "Who she wants me to end up with, and who I'm supposed to be with are two different things. Don't worry about it." He pulled away. "But I do need to take Theo to her so she'll stay out of our hair. Wait for me. I'll be back in a few."

Aspen turned and saw the spider woman scuttling across the floor. Her stomach churned. No, thank you. She made her way down the spiral staircase to the second floor. Aspen could barely get through the hallway. People were everywhere. She figured she could wait by the fire-eaters. They were far more entertaining than spider woman.

Easier said than done. The crowd wouldn't move. At the end of the hall, Aspen saw the fortuneteller talking to Tori. Aspen's heart twisted. How she wished Tori would talk to her again. Determined to make up with her, Aspen pushed her way through the crowd and found herself in the middle of several kids yelling "trick or treat" to a harried midget who was trying to control the line for the fortuneteller. Aspen found a chair and waited for Tori.

A short way down the hall stood Rowan. Next to him, laughing, was the most beautiful woman Aspen had ever seen. She had shoulder length platinum hair waved and curled to frame her heart-shaped face. Her smoky blue eyes never left Rowan's face.

The woman smiled, revealing perfectly straight, bright white teeth. She wore a blood-red strapless dress that revealed a tiny waist and flared out to her calves. And of course, the requisite three-inch black pumps. Aspen could never get away with wearing something like that. But women like her, women who belonged in a Victoria's Secret catalog, could. Why was she talking to Rowan? Probably waiting for a boyfriend or something.

Aspen was so enthralled with the Rowan/Hottie show, she nearly missed Tori when she came off the dais. Tori had gone with a traditional sexy French maid costume. A little cliché, but that was Tori.

"Tori, wait."

She spun around. "Oh, it's you. You'll have to excuse me. The fortuneteller didn't say anything about back-stabbing best friends, so I suppose we have no future."

"I'm sorry, and I miss you. Please talk to me."

She cocked her head. "No, I don't think so. A real friend wouldn't have done what you did. Excuse me. I need to find my date."

Tori disappeared down the hall, and Aspen watched, debating whether to go after her. She wondered who her date was. Probably a guy from Bozeman. Aspen wandered down the hall and decided it would be a good time to find Sid. She hadn't seen him since he went after Pearl. Aspen guessed his sister was giving him a hard time.

She stopped in front of the sword swallowers juggling their weapons. If she asked nicely, would they show her how to do it? Probably not, but she could talk to Vicki about it later. A finger traced the tattoo on her back. Aspen shivered. Then the hand lay flat and circled her belly drawing her back. It had to be Sid. But the smell was different. Vodka and sweat instead of cedar. Aspen's snake slithered out from her hair and hissed at her groper, who was probably one of the creepers Vicki hired. His hand slipped, and she moved away from him toward the swords.

Aspen didn't want to see who it was, because being violated, even mildly, reminded her too much of Marc. What a way to complete the horrid night. Not only had Sid's sister yelled at her and Tori still wasn't talking to her, now she had someone who thought they could put their hands all over her without invitation.

Her groper grabbed her hand and pulled her back. "Aspen, it's been too long," his slimy voice slurred in her ear. "Who knew I'd find you here? At my cousin's party no less. And looking like you want your clothes taken off. Come with me. Maybe you'll enjoy it this time."

Aspen froze. It *was* Marc. How was this possible? She thought it was just some creepy carny.

She took deep calming breaths and focused on her aikido training. Go with the attack, don't fight it. Go with the flow. Against her better judgment, she let Marc pull her toward him. When he had his arms wrapped around her, she adjusted, and he laughed thinking she was trying to get closer to him. But her adjustment was for her benefit, not his, since she'd have an easier time getting a grip on him this way. Aspen was shocked at how clear her mind was. Maybe Sid was having a good effect on her.

Marc moved her into a clearing with less people. Grabbing the hand that held her, she ducked and flipped him over her. He landed with a crash, and she ran. Aspen weaved through the crowd seeking one thing. The swords. Marc wouldn't assault her again. She'd kill him first.

Aspen saw him making his way toward her. She jumped onto the stage and waited. The sword swallower was still juggling. She waited for a sword to come close to the ground and grabbed it. She ran before he had a chance to stop her.

"Hey," he yelled. "Hey, get back here. Those are dangerous."

But Aspen didn't listen to him. Marc was close. As she shoved through the crowd, people muttered. Marc was yelling her name. Stupid oaf. As long as she could hear him, she could avoid him. Especially since he was obviously drunk. No way she would let him get close. The stairs were tricky. She didn't want to hurt anyone, but she needed to put space between Marc and herself. And she needed to find Sid, Theo, or Vicki. Marc wouldn't dream of attacking her if she were with someone. Though he didn't think twice over grabbing her in the crowd. Who knew what he would do.

Aspen kept the sword down and close to the wall as she wove down the stairs. "Aspen, Aspen. I see you." His voice rang out above the crowd. Once she was downstairs, it would be easier. Sid was down there. And her mom and dad. Thinking about it now, she realized how stupid it was for her not to tell them what happened. If she had, then she wouldn't be in this mess right now. He would be in jail.

The stairs gave way to another huge group of people. Aspen hurried into the entryway. She could no longer hear Marc yelling behind her. That was scarier, though, because she had no idea where he was. The smell of corn dogs and candied apples made her stomach turn.

"What's with the sword?" asked Vicki, who was standing near the front door.

"I stole it from the sword swallower. Don't ask."

Vicki opened her mouth to stay something, but another family walked in. She probably wouldn't be Aspen's best protection. The hallway cleared, and she saw Sid on the far side of the great room. He was arguing with his sister, but now Theo and Ella were with him, although Ella was busy playing with the cotton candy machine.

Aspen sighed from relief and made her way toward him. Sid wouldn't let anything happen to her. When she passed the stairs, a hand grabbed her arm. Marc pulled her into a cubbyhole under to the steps. She struggled, but the space was too tight, and she couldn't get the sword around.

"You can't even scream, because all the little kids are screaming. No one will think anything of a scream. This will be fun."

He placed a grimy hand on Aspen's stomach and slid it downward. Breathe and think. The sword was too big to bring up but she could drop it. She'd have to adjust a little more, which involved moving her body closer to the creep. Aspen moved her hand behind her and leaned into Marc. Then she thrust the sword down, hard. Marc howled. Target reached. She hoped she cut off a toe.

She pushed her way out of the cubby, ran down the hall and into the crowded living room. This time she didn't even look for Sid. She just ran. When she made her way around the crowd, Sid still stood there with his sister.

"Sid," Aspen hollered, grabbing his arm. "Sid, he's here."

"Who?"

"Marc. He's chasing me. Do you have security?"

Pearl brought her eyebrows up. "Is she talking about Marcellus?"

"Yes. And he's here. Theo, go with Raja and find him. Don't let him leave. Kill him if you have to but don't let him leave," said Sid.

"Sid, wait. You don't have to kill him. We can just call the police. Seriously. I don't want you guys going to jail."

She met his eyes, comprehension dawning. Marc was a dragon. That's what he meant by cousin. Unbelievable.

Sid put his hands on Aspen's shoulders. "Nothing's going to happen to us. But we are not letting him get away. I promise you."

Raja spoke up. "Where did you see him?"

Aspen pointed toward the cubbyhole. "I left him there. But he's probably disappeared by now."

Theo and Raja took off.

Sid dragged Aspen and Pearl up the stairs and into the empty theater room.

"You two wait in here. I'm going to go help Raja and Theo. We're going to catch this bastard."

Sid kissed her and ducked out of the room. Before the door shut all the way, Pearl's eyes widened.

"I have to put out my own fire. I'll be back in a second." Pearl grabbed the door handle.

"Please don't leave me," Aspen whispered.

"I told you that you were in over your head. You have no idea what's going on. Now I have to go, or things are going to get worse."

The door clicked shut, and Aspen walked to the couch and sank into the cool leather. A hand gripped her ankle, and she froze.

"You've got a mighty big secret here. One I think Obsidian wouldn't want coming out."

She jerked her foot out of his hand. "I don't know what you are talking about," she said.

Marc pulled at the leather band, and it came right off. "I saw you come in tonight."

Aspen looked into Marc's creepy eyes. He pulled himself up, wincing.

"You did a number to my foot. I can't walk very well. Imagine my luck when I remembered your little secret. I thought I was a dead man, but you may have just given me the ability to stay alive."

Aspen moved away from him.

"What do you mean?"

He laughed. "You mean you don't know? That tattoo means Obsidian has to die."

Aspen's heart clenched. Was that true? Obsidian had always said they had to be careful, but she didn't realize it meant he would die. On the off chance Marc was right, she had to play nice, or he would spill the beans.

"What do you want?" Aspen asked.

"I see you understand. First, I need you to get me safely out of here. Then I think you'll need to stay with me for a little while. Someone needs to nurse my foot back to health. Then my spirits will need lifting." He winked, and Aspen gagged.

He tried to put weight on his foot and winced.

"Come here." He waved her over and put his arm around her shoulder. It was all Aspen could do to not punch him in the nose. But he knew about their secret, which meant she had to cooperate. Plus, she was terrified to be alone in a room with him. Maybe out in public Sid would see them and take care of him.

"Wait," Aspen said and lightly pressed down on his foot with her own.

"What?" he growled.

"I'll go with you and help you with your foot, but we are not sleeping together again. If you even so much as try to touch to me, I'll break every one of your fingers. I learned how after our adventure in the woods. I could probably blind you too. Do you understand?"

Aspen pressed down a little harder, and he whimpered. "Okay, yes. Just get me out of here. If Sid and Theo catch me, I'm a dead man."

Aspen had no doubt about that.

He leaned on her as they wove in and out of the crowds. There was no sign of Sid, Theo, or Pearl. Aspen looked everywhere for them. That was her only hope. She didn't know what she would do if they made it outside.

As soon as they were clear of the door, Marc pointed to a black Mustang and handed her the keys.

"I can't drive," he said.

"Fair enough."

Aspen climbed into the driver's seat and took two deep breaths. She should run now, find Sid, and he could get Marc. Especially if Marc couldn't drive. Marc climbed into the passenger seat, pulled something out from underneath his seat, and pointed it at her.

"I figured you might need some additional persuading." Aspen didn't know much about guns, but that one looked scary.

"Where are we going?" she asked, her palms sweating.

"Into the park."

Aspen nodded. They drove about fifteen minutes and came to a large clearing.

"Here's good. Pull over and help me out."

Aspen did as he said, and he leaned on her while limping into the field, the gun still held in his other hand.

"Okay, stand back."

She backed up, and he collapsed on the ground. A few seconds later his body began to transform.

His arms became golden wings, his neck elongated, and he grew a long tail.

He looked down at her.

I should take you with me.

Aspen crossed her arms and backed up a little bit. *How do I know you won't spill the beans on Obsidian?*

He snorted, and gold colored smoke came out of his nostrils.

With you here, Obsidian will hang himself. I don't have to do that for him. Don't worry, though. After Obsidian is dead, I will come for you, and we'll spend a lot of time together.

He spread his wings and lifted off. Out of nowhere another golden dragon swooped down and drug his claws through Marc's wing. Marc roared, golden flames shooting from his mouth, and dropped to the ground.

Obsidian flew in from the other side and landed in front of Marc. He never looked so fierce before. He turned to look at Aspen.

This isn't safe. Get out of here.

She grabbed her phone and hid in a small stand of trees. She'd be able to get good pictures of whatever was about to go down.

CHAPTER 39

O BSIDIAN LOOKED AT the despicable creature in front of him who lay in a heap. He knew what he had to do, but that didn't mean he wanted to.

Your days are numbered, he said to Marc.

Marc snorted. *I could say the same about you, foolish king. That girl is going to be the death of us both.*

Don't blame Aspen for your crimes.

My crimes are minor compared to yours.

Good thing mine can be kept a secret.

No, I'm going to the council. They'll pardon me after I tell them about you.

Obsidian couldn't believe Marcellus actually thought he'd get away. He crept closer to Marcellus.

You aren't going to make it through the night.

Marcellus looked up at him, his eyes showing fear for the first time since Obsidian arrived.

Are you sure you want to kill me? I'm defenseless. I thought you were better than that. This isn't a fair fight.

This isn't a fight. This is me taking my position as king. I'm rendering judgment, and you've been found guilty.

Marcellus snorted. *What's my crime?*

Forcibly mating with a human girl.

Not a crime worth death.

It is actually, but that's not all. You've also been preying on innocent humans in Yellowstone. We do not eat human flesh. It's an abomination.

Wait? What are you—

Obsidian clamped his jaws around Marcellus's head, and with a powerful jerk, tore it from his body.

He dropped the head and backed away. He had to finish the job. Marcellus was dead, but he couldn't leave the body there. No dragon deserved the disgrace of decay, even wretched ones like Marcellus. He turned to Theo, who had been watching from the side.

Will you help me?

Of course.

They both opened their mouths and released the hottest fire they had. Obsidian's black flames mingled with Theo's gold. Within a few seconds all evidence of Marcellus's life was reduced to a pile of ash.

Obsidian turned to Theo.

I'm going to find Pearl and let her know that Marcellus has been taken care of. Do you mind going home?

Whatever you want. Good luck with Pearl. It's a good thing it's dark tonight.

Theo nodded toward Sid's ankle.

I'll explain later, said Sid.

Of course, Your Majesty.

CHAPTER 40

ASPEN WAITED UNTIL both dragons had disappeared before she crept out of her hiding place. She'd taken enough pictures to prove to the world that the dragons could police themselves. Now that Obsidian had killed Marc, she knew there would be no more dragon killings. It was a little terrifying seeing Obsidian attack Marc. She had to remember not to anger him while he was in dragon form.

She walked out to the middle of the field. Marc's glittering ashes were scattered around the grass. Aspen thought about touching it but just took pictures of instead. She didn't want to touch any part of Marc.

She heard a whoosh of wings behind her and looked up. In the moonlight the scales of a gigantic golden dragon sparkled. He flew low, and she adjusted her phone to capture him. She snapped away, but the setting wasn't quite right. She made a small adjustment on her camera and searched for him again. He was closer, maybe twenty feet away, and headed straight for her. At first she couldn't believe her luck, but as he got nearer, fear snuck into her heart. His jaws were wide open.

THE END

FROM THE AUTHOR

I HOPED YOU ENJOYED reading Obsidian. If you are interested in the next book in the series, it will be released in April 2016 and can be purchased here:

KimberlyLoth.com/aspen

Want to a free book? Click here to get the first book of my other series, The Thorn Chronicles absolutely free:

KimberlyLoth.com

If you enjoyed this book, or even if you didn't, please consider leaving a review. As an Indie author, reviews are crucial.

Thank you for reading!

ABOUT THE AUTHOR

K IMBERLY LOTH CAN'T decide where she wants to settle down. She's lived in Michigan, Illinois, Missouri, Utah, California, Oregon, and South Carolina. She finally decided to make the leap and leave the U.S. behind for a few years. She spent two wild years in Cairo, Egypt. Currently, she lives in Shenzhen, China with her husband and two kids. She is a middle school math teacher by day (please don't hold that against her) and YA author by night. She loves romantic movies, chocolate, roses, and crazy adventures. *Obsidian* is her sixth novel.

ACKNOWLEDGEMENTS

I T'S RARE THAT I discuss God in my books. I do this for a variety of reason. I write secular fiction. It can be career suicide if I offend the wrong person, so I usually keep my faith and my books completely separate. I'm sure as a reader you can sometimes see my faith come through, but I try to make sure that I don't preach (because I can't stand books that preach.)

But if I were to leave God out of these acknowledgements I would be doing a grave disservice. For you to understand what role he played in my career I have to back up. Seven years. I'm a Mormon. I believe in God. I believe in Jesus Christ. I believe in modern day prophets and apostles. Every six months I sit down for around twelve hours and listen to them speak (spread out over a weekend. Twelve hours all at once would be a little much.) Those two weekends are my favorite weekends of the year. In 2008, a talk was given by Dieter F. Uchtdorf. He's a German apostle and my favorite. He spoke about the fact that we are all creative beings because we are literal sons and daughter of the most creative being in the universe and to be happy we have to create also. That talk changed my life. (If you want to read the whole thing you can here: http://bit.ly/1grWXJJ). I started writing Obsidian the very next week and now I've finally published it. I thank God everyday that he inspires me and allows me to be creative in this way. I've never been happier.

I also want to publically thank God for bringing the following individuals into my life that helped in its creation.

Virginia and Leah: You two were the first to read it and without your feedback and cheers, I'm not sure I would've had the courage to continue.

Mandy, Kristin, and Karen: How long did we work on this thing together? Two years? Three? A lot. Thanks for being my team. Love you all more than you know.

Kate, Tiffany, Brittany, Chad, Holly, and others the others who beta read for me, thank you!

Will, Xandi and AJ: You three keep me sane and far more supportive than I've ever deserved. I have no words to express how grateful I am to have you in my life and tell you how much I love you.

Mom: Thanks for raising me in the faith. You've given me a lot over the years, but your testimony never ceases to amaze me and you've been my rock.

Matt: Thank you for challenging my faith. Without you I would've been blind to what I believed. You made sure I did my research. To this day I remember arguments we had when I was a kid and I'm always tickled when I find an answer.

Sarah, Suzi, and Kelly: Your editing skills are superb and I can't imagine how awful this would be without you.

Rebecca Frank: Holy cow girl! People are going to buy the book without even looking at the description because that cover is too amazing. Thank you!!!!

Colleen: With every book, I'm reminded why I love you so much. Thanks for making it look pretty.

My QSI family: Before I arrived, I didn't feel like a real author. Thank you for the opportunity to speak and show off my talent.

I would like to end this with publicly declaring my faith. Here is my testimony:

I believe I am daughter of God. He created this amazing universe in which we live and he wants nothing more than for me to be like him. As a parent, he knew I would struggle on this earth. He knew I would fall, but he also knew I would dust myself off and stand back up. Thousands of years ago he sent his first born son, Jesus Christ, to earth to die and more importantly, live again, so that I can also live again after I die. His words are written down in the bible and the Book of Mormon, another testament of Jesus Christ. He speaks today through modern day prophets and apostles. He also speaks to all of us through the Holy Ghost. I know that I will be with my family for eternity.

For more information on what I believe go to: Mormon.org.